SILENT KNIGHT

C R A I G L. C A R L S O N

Copyright © 2001 Col. Chev. Craig L. Carlson, KCTJ

ALL RIGHTS RESERVED. EXCEPT AS PERMITTED UNDER THE UNITED STATES COPYRIGHT ACT, 1976, NO PART OF THE PUBLICATION MAY BE REPRODUCED OR DISTRIBUTED IN ANY FORM OR BY ANY MEANS, OR STORED IN A DATA BASE OR RETRIEVAL SYSTEM, WITHOUT THE PERMISSION OF THE AUTHOR.

Library of Congress Cataloging-in-Publication Data

Carlson, Craig L.
    Silent Knight, – 1st ed.
       ISBN: 0-9654220-7-0

Published by:
Phoenix Press
P.O. Box 1899
Little Rock, Arkansas 72203-1899
U.S.A.

First Edition
10 9 8 7 6 5 4 3 2 1

For more information on the Silent Knight program, visit *www.TheSilentKnight.com*

*FOR MO,
MY HELENA.*

Colonel Chev. Craig L. Carlson, USA, KCTJ

Craig is a career Army officer with over twenty-three years of service to the nation. He has held every leadership position from Platoon Leader to Battalion Commander and has recently graduated from the National War College, Fort McNair, Washington, D.C.

Born in Austin, Texas in 1955 his earliest memories are of his father in starched khaki uniforms and World War II awards. Donald W. Carlson, his father, was Commandant and Dean of Boys at San Marcos Baptist Academy where he mentored and prepared young men and women for life. This experience shaped the author's life and values. There was never any doubt that Craig would pursue an Army career that would reflect the father he respected and loved.

His mother, Martha Carlson, has become Craig's hero. She rose to the challenge of providing for two of her three children after Donald became too debilitated from Parkinson's Disease to continue working. Martha, by the grace of God and great faith, was able to send her children to college and care for her husband until his death in 1987. She continues to be a blessing and inspiration.

The author is married to the former Monika (Mo) Conrady of Bitburg, Germany. According to Craig, she is the best decision he ever made. This book is dedicated to Mo, Craig's Helena.

Craig has two children, John (23) and Kara (19).

John was the inspiration for the young Squire depicted in this book.

Colonel Carlson has a B.S. Degree in Sociology from Texas A&M University, a Masters of Military Art and Science Degree from Fort Leavenworth, Kansas, and a Masters of National Security Strategy from the National Defense University. He has been published in *Military Review*, a military professional journal, and is an honorary member of the staff and faculty of the Army Command and General Staff College. He is an Honorary Kentucky Colonel and a Knight Commander in the Sovereign Military Order of the Temple of Jerusalem. His military awards include the Legion of Merit, Defense Meritorious Service Medal, Army Meritorious Service Medal with four oak leaf clusters, the Army Staff Badge and the Army Parachutist Badge.

ACKNOWLEDGEMENTS

The SILENT KNIGHT has been a labor of love. It is a deeply personal story that reflects many real events in my life. Names have been changed and some characters are composites of people I have known. A few are absolute fiction.

This book would not have been possible without the encouragement of my family and friends. I wish to convey my sincerest appreciation to the following persons for making a difference to me.

I was fortunate to grow in a Christian home. My parents, Donald and Martha Carlson, did the best job of parenting that I have known. The gift of confidence is one of immeasurable value. They taught, mentored, empowered and loved their kids.

My brother, Chriss Carlson, and my sister, Carol Thompson, were always there to read, reread or encourage.

Mike Murphy recommended Mo and me for knighthood in the Sovereign Military Order of the Temple of Jerusalem. Without that act of thoughtfulness the SILENT KNIGHT charity and book would not have happened.

Templar friends: Mark and Missie Bickham, Dale and Susan Leppard, Marshall (my editor) and Pam Bachman were always there for advice or encouragement. Marshall's editing talent is a gift from God. His timing was perfect. David Wooten worked the magic to make the book real. His enthusiasm came at the right time.

Role models that shaped my life: teachers, preachers, soldiers, leaders, and too many others to name here. Many of you know who you are, some I need to tell before it is too late. Many are reflected in the following chapters.

RADM James Carey immediately backed the SILENT KNIGHT charity concept. He put his reputation and considerable influence behind it. It is largely to ADM Carey's desire to make a difference for humanity that this book and the charity are real. A mere thank you is not enough. He has a friend for life.

Finally, there is Mo. No man could ask for a better partner. She made me believe I could write. Now, I hope my readers believe it too.

FOREWORD

When Col. Carlson first asked me to read the draft version of the first three chapters of this book, I put it in my briefcase as "airplane reading" where I could digest it without telephone interruptions and other distractions. One week later, I was on a flight to Dallas and pulled it out of my briefcase and began reading. I was immediately intrigued and more accurately "hooked."

This story came to life for me as I was drawn into the character of the retired U.S. Army Colonel who uses his position as a Knight in the Sovereign Military Order of the Temple of Jerusalem [The Knights Templar] to do good for others less fortunate, and further uses those good deeds as the catalyst to train young men [and later young ladies] about the personal satisfaction and wonderful feeling of service to mankind that comes from such acts of the heart. I couldn't put the draft copy down until I'd read it twice.

I called Col. Carlson from Dallas to ask when I could read the rest of the book? That opportunity came three months later when he completed the final draft. Once again, I read the final version on an airplane, this time on the way to Europe. I freely confess that parts of it made me, a grown and retired military man, cry with tears of joy at the absolute goodness that was being achieved by this kind and caring Silent Knight. I could identify with the main character, Colonel Peterson, who had first served his nation in combat and mortal danger, and was now, with the strong support of a wonderful life's companion and wife, using his maturity, experience and leadership to pass along the wonderful feeling of fulfillment and serenity gained from simply and anonymously helping one's fellow and less fortunate citizens meet their individual needs.

Col. Carlson, as the author of *Silent Knight*, has truly identified something in the soul of mankind that causes many of us to seek a greater good than simply the standard pursuit of material things for our families and selves. He has found an inner sanctum that not everyone can describe; but a quiet and peaceful security within oneself that comes from wanting to do something to make the lives of complete strangers better for the simple reason that it's the right thing to do. And to do so anonymously, not seeking thanks or personal aggrandizement, but rather the simple satisfaction of having done something good that has made the life of another better for one shining moment.

I feel we are all fortunate that he has taken the time to put these thoughts and concept in written form where it can be shared with others, and where you, the reader, can, as I did, experience the absolute and unselfish goodness that mankind can exhibit if only given the tools of an honorable life and the desire to make ours a better world for everyone, and not just those who are in our immediate families.

I am honored to have been given the opportunity to read this book before publication, and to share my thoughts with Col. Carlson, and to be further honored by being asked to provide this Foreword as my small part of this magnificent effort. If this book encourages just one human being to do just one kind thing for another human being, then it will have been both successful and a living memorial to all things good in the Eyes of God. And if it encourages hundreds or thousands to do so and to do so anonymously, so much more the better to carry out the motto of The Knights Templar, which is *NON NOBIS DOMINE, NON NOBIS, SED NOMINI TUO DA GLORIAM,* "Not Unto Us, Oh Lord, Not Unto Us, But To THY NAME Give Glory".

This book, through its main character, the old Colonel, carries out that motto each and everyday, and it is indeed a superb example for all of us to follow. I intend to emulate The Colonel, and by so doing, make ours a better world and my life a better example for those who follow in my footsteps to make our planet, truly, a place where each of us cares more about others than we do our own personal comforts.

God Bless All Who Read These Words,

Rear Admiral [Ret.] James J. Carey, GCTJ, GMTJ
  International Grand Commander of The Knights Templar

SILENT KNIGHT

CHAPTER 1

Colonel (Retired) Donald Wilhelm Peterson was sixty-five with an elegant stature and well-groomed appearance. On first glance, he had an aura of having led an active life. The surrounding décor of the room would validate that opinion. As a retired officer of Artillery with thirty years of active service the large living room where he stood was well stocked with military memorabilia, antiques, lithographs and plaques arranged on the dark oak walls. The Persian carpets and fine leather chairs further alluded to some degree of financial comfort. He seemed content watching the fireplace, which cast a lovely orange glow about the room and made his facial lines more pronounced in the fading evening light. His hair was white and receding, the face was kindly with eyes that had a pleasant spark and hinted of a deeper knowledge.

His thoughts were about the young men that had served him over the past twenty years as Squires and their memory was very special to him. A new one was to arrive any minute and the anticipation was a good feeling. What would this one be like? Would he be as good as the others? Was the Colonel getting too old to

SILENT KNIGHT

relate to this generation? Father Riley had a good sense about the character and moral fiber of the young men he had recommended but there was always this nagging anticipation.

The young man who approached the house wore a blue button-down collared shirt, a navy blue sweater and khaki pants. His black hair was unruly and was further disheveled by the cool fall breeze that crossed the well-manicured lawn. The boy thought, it was cold for September, but 1985 had been a strange year for weather. His 16-year-old face was creamy with red child-like cheeks. He did not look comfortable. The clothes were not of his choosing and he tugged at them with obvious disapproval. John Conrady had no idea what awaited him and he felt as though he had been summoned to the principal's office for punishment. As he rang the doorbell, he had an almost overwhelming inclination to run away.

The Colonel opened the door and fixed his trained eyes on the young man's face. It amused him as he thought about how the squires seemed to get younger looking every year. It is funny how age changes your perception of youth. The young man had a childlike face pure and innocent.

"You must be Squire John... I have been expecting you. Father Riley called to say he had spoken to your parents and that you would be dropping by this evening. Together, we are going to do much good. It is a pleasure to meet

SILENT KNIGHT

you. Father Riley has many good things to say about you."

As Donald extended his hand, he smiled warmly and in a disarming way motioned for John to enter the house.

John was relieved by the brief introduction and warmed by the gentleman's manner; he timidly shook Donald's hand. He had not one clue as to the meaning of the "Squire" reference.

"Yes, sir, I am John Conrady. My father told me that I should drive here this evening and that you would explain some... job... you want me to volunteer for."

The young man scanned the vestibule and into the living room at the assembled memorabilia and art. To him, the house looked more like a museum than a home. It was not intimidating... but it was different from any home he had seen.

"That is correct. First, can I fix you a soda or tea?"

"A Coke would be fine."

They moved into the kitchen and poured two glasses and walked back to the living room where they sat opposite each other. The lesson began...

"John, you are the eighteenth Squire I have enlisted for service. Do you know what a Squire is?"

John was perplexed... he wondered where this conversation was leading.

"No, sir."

SILENT KNIGHT

"A Squire is a Knight's apprentice and helper. You see, I belong to an Order of Christian Knights that seeks to do good for people in need. We prefer to be anonymous, as we do not seek recognition for our random acts of charity. That is where you come in. As my Squire, I will enlist your support one or two days a month to run charitable errands for me."

John looked at Donald and thought, this man isn't playing with a full deck. He must be deluding himself. This talk about Knights and Squires... crazy. He said, "Why do you want to be anonymous?"

"Because the Order's motto is "Not unto us, Oh Lord, not unto us, but to Thy Name give glory." We do these things for God... not for ourselves. This is why you will deliver the gifts, and I will remain a "silent knight." That is your mission, to maintain my anonymity. As a matter of fact, this charity is referred to, within the Order, as Silent Knight."

John was searching for something to say. He thought the Colonel was crazy and that this would be the last time he would see this man, but John was not bold enough to say so. What came out was:

"Well, Sir, that doesn't sound too difficult. Why me?"

"Your family priest, Father Riley, and I are friends and we have worked together for several years identifying young men for duty as Squires. His judgment has been flawless... and I suspect you will prove to be a noble Squire."

SILENT KNIGHT

Donald looked at John and asked him, "Do you want to help me do some good?"

John felt trapped. Thought the idea was pretty strange, but now he had to respond.

"How long will I be a Squire?"

"For only one year in active service; however, your name will be added to my cherished list and you will always be my Squire."

A year, when you are just sixteen, sounds more like a punitive sentence than a limit and Donald could sense the young man's thoughts.

"Well, Squire John... do you accept?"

John had to commit. It was a good cause, how could he not say yes. Maybe he could say yes and never show up again. That was a possible option. Trapped! No escape!

"Yes sir... it sounds... interesting... but... do you have to call me Squire? My friends might think it was kind of weird."

"No... if the title bothers you... I will just call you John."

"When do we start?"

"First, I have something for you."

The Colonel reached into his pocket and withdrew a lapel pin and attached it to the young man's collar.

"This pin has the cross of the Order on the white shield of a Knight. The sword through the center represents our knightly heritage and the "SK" stands for the program Silent Knight. It is to be worn whenever you are performing Silent Knight activities. It is to remind you that you are to conduct yourself in a manner that

SILENT KNIGHT

would make those you represent proud."

The new Squire felt the pin, smiled and thought this was pretty cool. He had seen only one other kid wearing one at church and had wondered what it meant. That kid was now graduating from college and being commissioned as an Army lieutenant.

Next, the Colonel took a business card and wrote his home phone number on it and handed it to John.

"You have direct access to me. If I can help you or if you know someone that needs help, you may call me. You have friends in your school, look beyond them and find the ones that need confidence or a little boost. Maybe we can make a difference for someone. If I can assist you with advice or with a recommendation, do not hesitate to call. You are welcome in this house and I hope that you will feel comfortable as we get to know each other better. My wife, Helena, is a Dame within the Order and she is well aware of Silent Knight business. She can answer questions if I am not available. I wish she were here this evening to meet you, but she is helping another friend of ours."

"What should I call you?"

"I have been called many things in my life. You may call me Don, Donald, Colonel or anything you are comfortable with, as long as you are smiling."

The Colonel winked at John and both grinned at each other.

"Now, you are ready for your first mission. I

have a couple of bags of groceries in the kitchen for you to deliver to Mrs. Robertson, she lives at 1004 East Oak Street. She is widowed, elderly and has difficulty taking care of herself. She has no family and has little income. She used to volunteer at the Methodist Church and took care of her husband until he died two years ago of Parkinson's Disease."

The young man thought that this was too quick; no way out! He started looking through the bags. There were many canned items, some easy TV dinners, instant soups, some fresh baked cookies, a couple of bars of candy, toilet paper, soap, new sponges, a hair brush and a small bottle of cologne. There was no doubt that this would be a welcome gift.

"This is a nice thing to do and should be very easy."

"John, there is more... take this envelope and hand it to Mrs. Robertson, it is addressed to her. Inside is an anonymous card with our Order's Crest and motto. Tell her that you were asked to deliver some groceries. If she asks who they are from, or insists that they are not hers, tell her that the items are from an Order of Christian Knights that recognize her service to the community and wish to do something for her. If she invites you in, set the groceries in the kitchen and politely wish her a good evening and depart. If she doesn't invite you in, ask where she would like the items left."

"OK. Seems easy enough."

Donald reached into his pocket and pulled

SILENT KNIGHT

out a five-dollar bill.

"Here, this is for you."

John looked at the bill and said, "I shouldn't take money for this. This is voluntary."

"The money is for your expenses... gas for your car. You should not have any expenses while serving as my Squire. It is not an option... it isn't much, take it."

John tucked the money in his pocket, wrestled the groceries to his car and departed for Mrs. Robertson's house.

The Colonel waved and wished him well on his first mission. Silently he prayed that John would learn much from this experience.

The new Squire pulled his 1980 Jeep Grand Wagoneer to the curb in front of a rundown wooden cottage that must not have seen new paint in at least twenty years. The yard was overgrown with English ivy that appeared to have swallowed the mailbox standing next to the curb. The house was dark except for the light projected from a television set in the front room. He checked his watch as he approached the front door, it was 7:00 pm. He felt uncomfortable and wanted to get this over with as fast as possible. Through an old window screen and sheers, he could make out the figure of an old woman sitting in front of a television. From the volume, he assumed Mrs. Robertson was quite deaf. It took two heavy knocks to rouse her. He watched as she looked from her chair toward the door, reached for her cane and

SILENT KNIGHT

struggled to her feet. It must have taken her two minutes to cover the short distance. She seemed bent and crippled with arthritis.

Mrs. Robertson opened the heavy front door, which was behind an old screen door and inquired, "Who is it?" Her voice was an airy whisper of a person that had been in a long struggle, but the sound was pleasantly high pitched and musical. Her bent back gave the impression that she was much smaller than she was.

"I am John Conrady, ma'am. I was asked to deliver some groceries to you at this address. Here is a card for you."

Mrs. Robertson opened the screen and took the card.

"Well! Who would do such a kind thing for me?"

"Ma'am, there is an Order of Christian Knights that wanted you to have these.

Where can I set them?"

Mrs. Robertson turned on the porch light and looked at John in a cautious way. John just wanted to get it over without being rude.

"Come in and set them on the kitchen table."

John entered the house and noted that it had a musty smell of old carpets and drapes. The house was simple, decorated with a few inexpensive pieces of porcelain and needed a good dusting. The kitchen sink had several unwashed dishes in it that had been there a few days. There was a half-eaten candy bar and half a jar of peanuts on the counter. Mrs. Robertson

SILENT KNIGHT

was wearing a simple housedress that had been worn far too often and she had a frayed sweater draped over her shoulders to keep the fall chill from her small frame. The house felt cold. He set the groceries on the table and nearly crushed Mrs. Robertson's gray cat that had been lounging there. It escaped the disaster with a loud yowl. John had been quite startled, but more amused than frightened.

The elderly woman scolded the cat in her quiet voice, while shaking a crooked finger in its direction. She muttered something about cats not being allowed on the kitchen table.

In the light of the kitchen Mrs. Robertson began looking into the bags while John started taking things out and setting them on the table. Mrs. Robertson looked at each item as if it were a Christmas present, but a lovely smile came to her face when she came to the cologne. She looked up, clutching the bottle, and said, "Oh! This is wonderful, I haven't had a new bottle of cologne since Raymond died." A tear ran down her cheek as she opened it and sniffed the fragrance.

"It smells lovely!"

She dabbed a little on the back of her hand.

John was immediately afraid he was going to cry. Mrs. Robertson looked so frail but the change in her mood from a depressed air to the lady standing before him with radiant eyes was remarkable. It struck him deep within his soul and he had to turn away. That so simple an act could bring such a feeling of joy was an awesome thought.

"Let me do these few dishes and help you put the groceries away, ma'am?"

The dishwashing was something he never would have volunteered to do, but he had to hide his face. He was embarrassed.

"Oh, you are so kind. I will fix us a soda."

"Please, don't go to any trouble, I really can't stay but a minute."

"I never have company and you are a very kind young man... I want to do something for your kindness too. Have a soda with me... please."

John had gotten his emotions in check but his eyes welled up and would not stop.

Every word that came from this lady somehow captured his heart. He had come on an errand and was now embarrassing himself by getting involved... and now she was wanting to give him something back. Something simple, but thoughtful. This was sad, tragic, lovely, kind and beautiful all rolled into one incredible experience. The emotions kept swelling as his heart went out to this frail old woman.

Soon he had cleaned the counter, too, and was working on dusting the pictures and table. The refrigerator was shockingly empty and what was there was old with many jars sealed with plastic and rubber bands. The smell was not fresh either... it took him awhile to clean it.

Mrs. Robertson had initially fussed about the boy cleaning up, but John said that every-

SILENT KNIGHT

body needs a little help now and then, and it would only take a minute. It was easier for him to do it than her. She had agreed with his simple logic.

Mrs. Robertson was now sitting at the dining room table still clutching the cologne and talking about Raymond. She would laugh and her eyes would dance and John just kept cleaning, occasionally commenting or laughing at something she would say. He was afraid to sit and look at her. It was more than he could bear. The lady's spirit seemed to rally as she lost herself in old stories. The airy whisper of a voice seemed to have found some source of power that somehow made the old woman John had met at the door become a little younger in his estimation. She was truly enjoying herself and his company.

She talked about her first date with Raymond... in a horse-drawn buggy! They were going to a revival... but the horse had been eating clover and.... She laughed till she had more tears running down her face. It was a great story and John had found himself laughing as much at Mrs. Robertson's pleasure as his own. She heaped praise on John for every little thing he would do, from dusting to replacing a burned-out bulb. He was not accustomed to hearing so many compliments or being so appreciated.

John finished his second soda and departed Mrs. Robertson's, assuring her that he would come visit again sometime. They parted as old

SILENT KNIGHT

friends and it was difficult to leave her, knowing that this was probably the only company she had had in her home in months... she was a kind, lonely woman that needed a friend.

Her final words to him were, "God bless you for your kindness." She had watched him drive away from the porch of her home.

John cried all the way home; he never felt better about himself in his life. It was 9:15 pm.

The next morning, as John prepared for school, he slipped on the funky clothing common to his peers and was about to leave when he spotted the lapel pin. He removed it from the collar of the shirt and looked at it. He thought he would take it with him to school. He placed it on the T-shirt but it didn't seem right. John carefully removed the pin and placed it in his pocket. All day, he would find the pin and study it and remember Mrs. Robertson's transformation. He walked a little taller, a little prouder and realized, he too had had a transformation. That evening, he called Colonel Peterson.

"Sir Donald... this is John Conrady... your Squire."

"Yes, John."

"Please call me Squire, Sir."

"Of course, Squire. What else can I do for you?"

"Nothing, Sir. I just felt I should call you. You made Mrs. Robertson very happy."

"No Squire... WE made Mrs. Robertson happy. Thank you for doing your part well.

SILENT KNIGHT

Let's do it again soon."

"Yes, Sir. I look forward to it."

As the Colonel hung up, he smiled and turned to his bride of twenty-five years and said with a wink, "This one will do."

SILENT KNIGHT

CHAPTER 2

Three weeks had gone by when John was summoned back to the Colonel's home.

He had been very excited about the Squire duty and was anxious to see what Sir Donald had in mind for the next mission. He remembered the first time he had come to their home... the feeling of discomfort because of the clothes his parents had told him to wear and the fear of the unknown. Now, the clothes and the pin were like a uniform and he felt like he had a purpose. It was good.

Mrs. Peterson answered the door. She was a lovely woman who had style and grace. Helena was what some men would refer to as a "Rolls Royce" or classic figure. This was not lost on John; even as a young man, he knew a beauty when he met one. The outfit she wore was not expensive nor was the jewelry she wore, she seemed to have an understated charm about her. The eyes were big, bright, brown and intelligent. She too had a spark that could not be missed. She carried her sixty years well.

"Squire John. Putzi has told me about you. He is very pleased."

John was surprised... Putzi!? She couldn't

15

SILENT KNIGHT

possibly be talking about Sir Donald.

"That is good to hear, ma'am. Who is Putzi?"

She laughed and said, "Donald, of course. I call him Putzi."

John smiled but could not visualize Sir Donald as Putzi.

The Colonel entered the living room wearing pressed blue jeans and a soft navy blue shirt. He wore reading glasses with gold wire rims. The book under his arm was "The Last Full Measure," a thick volume about the American Civil War. He smiled as he realized the two had enjoyed some little joke and seemed to be harboring a secret. He had to ask what they were smiling about.

"What are you two up to already? I can tell there is mischief in the air."

"Sir, you do not strike me as a Putzi!"

"Oh! Humor at my expense." The Colonel feigned disapproval.

"My bride has a charming way of humanizing me. It keeps my feet on the floor. When others call me Colonel or Sir Donald, I could get pretty full of myself. Nobody is intimidated by a man called "Putzi." It seems to amuse everyone that knows us. She calls me Putzhole when she isn't happy."

That really tickled John. They all laughed.

"Well, Helena has prepared some pasta and we can talk over dinner."

The meal was served in a formal setting. It was simple, elegant and had candles! John had never dined in this manner and worried about

SILENT KNIGHT

spilling something. To him, this was a very formal dinner. After the Colonel said the prayer, the salad was served from a silver bowl. He ate with the silverware that the hosts used and followed their lead. He drank mint iced tea... and loved it, while the Petersons enjoyed a glass of dark red wine. John looked over the table and around the room, and thought, "I would like to live like this someday."

The pasta was store-bought, but the sauce was homemade and had a lot of garlic and other flavors that John didn't recognize but certainly enjoyed. The desert was yogurt, honey and walnuts. At first he refused, but tried it and found the sweet and sour flavor very pleasing. He cleaned his plate. Conversation during dinner was humorous with many little stories about various experiences, families and friends. By the end of dinner, any inhibitions the Squire had started with seemed thoroughly dismissed.

"Squire John, I have a mission for you. Tomorrow, you are to take another envelope to school with you. The principal informed me several months ago that a young man had been unable to afford his class ring. We ordered it and paid for it. I want you to deliver the card with the ring. It must be done so the young man is not embarrassed. So pick your time well. Mr. Lucas, the principal, will have the ring for you and is expecting you."

"Which student is it?"

"It is Kenneth Pendleton."

SILENT KNIGHT

"I know him. His family is very poor. He doesn't have many friends, but he is a good guy... very quiet."

"Good! So finding him won't be any problem."

"No, Sir. He's in my Physical Education class three days a week."

"Wonderful! Can you do it without drawing attention to yourself or embarrassing him?"

"I can do it. You will be pleased."

"That's the spirit! I like that. I can see you are going to be one of my finest Squires."

John smiled at the compliment and felt proud to be a part of these... how did he state it? "Random acts of charity."

The three bonded very well that evening. Even the music the Petersons played was enjoyable. Perhaps a little old fashioned, but it fit them well and created a warm environment. Gentle jazz is what they called it. The Petersons were easy to be with and had many interesting stories. They spoke about their former Squires as if they were members of their family and remained in touch with all but one whom they seemed to miss. It appeared he had died suddenly. John did not feel comfortable pursuing his curiosity about it and the Petersons did not volunteer any information. The Colonel took great pleasure in answering questions about the military memorabilia he had collected. In the back yard he had been introduced to Ruprecht, the Petersons' puppy, a frisky Blue Merle Australian Shepherd. He was named for

SILENT KNIGHT

the Steve Martin character from the movie "Dirty Rotten Scoundrels" because of his lack of manners. The dog was playful and spoiled rotten. The couple seemed to really worship each other and laughed at themselves or shared cute barbs throughout the evening. The young Squire departed about 9:00 pm and was surprised he had been there for three hours.

The next morning, John wore a collared shirt and a fresh pair of jeans to school.

He had been wanting to wear his lapel pin to school and this was his first chance. It was displayed proudly on the pocket of his shirt.

His appearance was new to his friends. They joked with him about trying to look like a teacher; however, the teachers and principal were very complimentary and a few people asked about the pin. He wasn't prepared to talk about the pin and had responded that it was from a charitable Christian organization that he was involved with. That seemed to shock some of his friends; those that knew he attended the Catholic Church were not surprised and pursued it no further. John was feeling pretty self-conscious about his appearance when the neatest thing happened. Patti Filmore, one of the most popular girls in school, spoke to him. She had never noticed him before... and when her deep blue eyes had locked on his, wow! She knew my name! The encounter was brief, exhilarating and mind numbing. It took him several minutes to gather his wits. John's friends were equally amazed

SILENT KNIGHT

by Patti's apparent interest.

Girls had never had much to do with John. Not being blessed with great athletic ability or rugged good looks, plus being a rather shy personality didn't help. The Squire thought he had a baby face that didn't make him very appealing... and in the informal school hierarchy of importance, John was a "nobody." He had worked to be accepted by his peers... dressing and acting like them. It was the cool thing to do... and being accepted is everything to a teenager. Peer pressure is the strongest force acting on teens, more powerful than gravity or the need for air. Now, by catching the eye of Patti Filmore, he became a "somebody" to his peers. If John's ego were stock options, his friends were buying. It was a good day to be John Conrady!

At Physical Education the boys were showering and the lockers were open. John slipped the card and ring box into Kenneth's locker and cruised to the showers. When he finished, he moved back to his locker and observed the young man while dressing.

As Kenneth Pendleton was putting on his shirt he could not stop thinking about how humiliating it was going to be this afternoon when everyone *except him* got their senior ring. Everyone would be showing them off, and the fact that he didn't have one would be obvious. It would be just another embarrassment in a long line of embarrassments due to his family's poverty. This was a low point in his life and his

SILENT KNIGHT

stomach churned as he dwelled on it. He wished he could stop the earth from moving forward so he could avoid this impending personal tragedy.

His parents were deeply sorry, and he could see it in their eyes... they felt his pain. He loved them too much to say anything once they decided they could not afford the $235 necessary to order the ring.

As he reached for his shoes he noticed the envelope and for an instant thought he was in the wrong locker. Then he thought someone might be playing a trick on him. He looked around but nobody seemed to be paying any attention. The envelope was taped to a box, and was addressed to him... he opened it. The Crest on the outside of the card was colorful and impressive with SILENT KNIGHT written below it in bold letters. Again, Kenneth checked to see who was watching... nobody. He opened the card and read, "Not unto us, not unto us, O Lord, but to Thy Name give glory." A note was scribbled on the left-hand side that simply said, "Ken, you have integrity and lots of potential. Be well."

Again, he looked carefully around the dressing room. Nobody was laughing or appeared to be watching. This was strange. He opened the box and a brand new senior ring sat there like a heavy stone. He knew this was some sick joke. Again, he looked around the room for a prankster... nobody. He pulled the ring out and sure enough, "Ken Pendleton" was engraved

SILENT KNIGHT

on the inside. He sat down on the locker room bench with all his weight... as if he couldn't believe what was happening. He placed the ring on his finger and held it up. It fit. He smiled a huge toothy grin, looked around the room again... nobody paid any attention. The impact hit him. Somebody cared! Somebody saw his pain and helped him. He leaned forward placed his head in his hands and said, "Thank you, God." and wept. Nobody noticed but Squire John.

Kenneth must have read the card a hundred times over the next week.

Unobtrusively, the Squire had watched the event unfold and was pleased with his unnoticed delivery. The feeling he had was similar to the evening at Mrs. Robertson's: A wonderful satisfaction in knowing he had played a part in doing something good. He loved his part in this new drama. He wondered how many other Silent Knights were performing "random acts of charity." The thought crossed his mind... maybe I will be a Silent Knight someday.

That afternoon he called Sir Donald and reported his successful delivery. The Colonel could not have been more pleased. John could tell the Colonel really liked him... they had crossed an invisible line... they were friends. John had never had a friend that was nearly fifty years his senior. It was different and special. But, as he reflected on it, everything that had happened to him since becoming a Squire seemed to affect him more intensely. It was as if John had been walking in the dark and suddenly the lights were on. He sensed he was growing and it was good.

SILENT KNIGHT

CHAPTER 3

The Colonel's car had been in need of tire rotation. He had delivered his navy blue Lincoln Continental about an hour ago and was returning from a cigar shop a short walk from the auto repair house. He was quite pleased with himself. He had found the Macanudos he particularly enjoyed... and at a fair price. His years in the military had caused him to detest waiting in lines. There had always been lines: the Commissary, the medical clinics, the Post Exchange, the dining facilities, heck, you even had to wait in line to jump out of airplanes! Waiting at the repair shop thoroughly annoyed him; therefore, the proximity to the cigar shop was quite good fortune. The walk had been brisk and the fall air was clean and crisp. The cool air had stung his nose as he breathed it in... winter was coming. He had always enjoyed the changing seasons and the decorations that heralded the next holiday shopping spree. Today, the Halloween décor was being taken down and soon the Thanksgiving décor would replace it.

As he entered the tire store, he couldn't help noticing a young woman with two small children. She was totally occupied with corralling

SILENT KNIGHT

the young ones. Both were very animated little boys who appeared to be about two and four. The four-year-old was climbing through tire displays while the two-year-old sat in his mother's lap screaming with apparently his very best effort. The woman was tired and by her appearance was having trouble meeting the demands placed on young mothers.

When the Colonel arrived at the service counter, a man in his early twenties was being told that the two front tires on his truck would have to be replaced at a cost of ninety-five dollars before he would pass State inspection. The customer had the look of a mechanic... strong, dirty hands and clothing to match that impression. The clerk kept repeating that he couldn't get the price any lower. The young man was desperately explaining that he had no money for new tires and that he had to have the truck to get to work or he would lose his job. The elderly male clerk was not impressed and dismissed the man, saying it wasn't his problem.

The customer turned and walked back to the lady with the active kids. From across the room, Donald could not hear the conversation but the facial expressions and gestures were unmistakable disappointment. The couple was gathering their children, backpacks, toys and purse when the clerk handed the Colonel the bill for his tire rotation and the keys to the Lincoln.

"Sir, your car is ready. Here are your keys."

As Donald wrote the check, he added ninety-five dollars to the amount and informed the

SILENT KNIGHT

clerk of his intentions to pay for the previous customer's repair.

"You related to them, mister?"

"No, never saw them before."

The clerk looked at Donald like he was from another planet. The Colonel pulled a card from his coat breast pocket, jotted a note in the left facing page, and quickly put the card back in its envelope.

"I want a separate receipt for the two tires."

"Yes, Sir." The clerk shook his head. "I never seen anyone do this before."

"That is unfortunate. I would have hoped this would happen more often."

"You a preacher?"

"No... just another proud AARP (American Association of Retired Persons) member."

"Me, too."

Donald grinned at his backfired humor.

When the clerk produced the receipt, the Colonel placed it inside the card and sealed the envelope.

"I'll catch up with that family and send them back to you. Don't tell them who paid for it. It will be our secret."

The clerk smiled, "I'll be damned! I won't say a word."

"Thank you, friend. Have a good day."

The couple had moved to the vehicle return area and was now waiting with two squalling kids. The young mother was barely containing her own emotions and the father was staring at the ground with his hands shoved deep

27

SILENT KNIGHT

in his pockets.

The Colonel briskly walked up to the dejected young man, handed him the envelope, and said, "Sir, I believe you left this on the counter. The clerk asked me to give it to you."

The young man took the envelope with a quizzical look at Donald and stated, "There must be a mistake."

"I don't think so. Talk to the clerk."

With that, Donald walked to his car and drove away, the couple disappearing in his rearview mirror.

The father turned the envelope over and saw "Yes, this is yours." written across the front. He thought, this is strange and looked around a couple of times before he opened the envelope. The card had a colorful crest and "SILENT KNIGHT" written under it. Inside, the inscription read, "Not unto us, O Lord, not unto us, but to Thy Name give glory." On the left facing page was hand printed, "God cares about you. Enjoy the new tires." The receipt fell out and fluttered to the pavement. The young man grabbed for it, missed and it fluttered another ten feet before finally being captured under his right foot. He read it and again looked around.

His wife asked, "What is it now, Marty?"

"Sarah, you ain't gonna believe this. Our tires are paid for."

"What? You're kidding?"

He handed her the receipt.

"Who paid for it?"

"God."

SILENT KNIGHT

"What!"

"Read the card, Sarah."

She shifted the two-year-old to her left arm and examined the card.

"Marty, this is incredible! I had just prayed for help."

"You're kidding!"

"No! It's true. I had prayed on our way out of the shop that God would help us."

"This is too weird."

"Who gave you the card?"

"I don't know."

"You got a card from God and you weren't paying attention! Marty, it could have been an Angel!"

"This is really weird!"

"No... it isn't weird. My Grandmother always told me that God answered prayers. Now, I believe it."

As she hugged her husband's arm and moved back toward the waiting room, she said, "Thank you, God."

"Sarah, we are going to church on Sunday. It's been too long."

Later that evening, the Colonel and Helena sat on pillows in front of the fireplace, sipping sherry, and remembering other fires and younger times. They held each other and talked about their day. Donald always enjoyed relating his "Silent Knight" adventures to his bride. She was his favorite audience.

SILENT KNIGHT

SILENT KNIGHT

CHAPTER 4

Reverend Tyrone Wilson was a retired full gospel minister. He retired at 82 when his voice could no longer carry the Lord's message to the back row of the church. It was a small African-American church with a superb choir and Bible thumping charismatic preaching. The congregation of the church had been built on the love that Brother Wilson had nurtured. In fact, he had personally baptized most of the members and had helped birth another dozen. He had literally saved many lives from the hands of drug dealers and other disreputable persons that preyed on his beloved neighborhood. He was a deeply spiritual man that prayed in tongues and believed in the power of God. Tyrone was a role model for the community. Every deed and every word that he uttered was measured as if he were in the presence of the Lord. Reverend Wilson lived in the love of God and had led a miraculous life. At his current age of 90, the Spirit was still upon him, and in his company you could sense the power of God. Reverend Wilson's spirit was willing but his earthly body was growing weak and a wheel chair was now required to move him from his tiny apartment two blocks to the church. The

SILENT KNIGHT

lack of a wheel chair ramp required four men to lift this robust elderly man down one flight of twelve steps and back up each Sunday, Wednesday, and Thursday to attend church services.

Reverend Wilson was the eighth son of a farmer that lived on a forty-acre farm outside of Atlanta, Georgia. His father was the son of former slaves and Tyrone remembered his Grandfather, Theo, with great affection. A simple man by today's standard, but smart in the word of God. It was Theo that had inspired Tyrone to preach the Word. When his Grandfather had died at the not-so-tender age of one hundred three, the young reverend had personally dug his grave with a small Army shovel. Tyrone Wilson had come a long way in his life and worked for everything he had made of himself. His achievements were awesome in terms of their significance to his community; however, he had been a river to his people and church. As he put it, "I would have been more concerned about money had I known I would live this long." Three of the twelve stained glass windows in his old church were the product of Reverend Wilson's benevolence. His charity was legendary among his flock.

Tyrone no longer had peers; he had outlived them all. The people he had depended on to get him to and from Church were aging, and the climb up and down the stairs was becoming a dangerous senior citizen event. When the church attempted to purchase a wheel chair

SILENT KNIGHT

ramp, the cost of permits, labor, materials, zoning criteria and inspection requirements had placed the option out of reach. Indeed, the city and county bureaucracy had killed the project by red tape; no malice intended, just more local government out of control.

When Reverend Wilson had departed for church this morning, two of the four elders were breathing so hard by the time they reached the bottom step that Tyrone would have started last rites for each of them had he been a Catholic. The four men had their coats off and were trying to safely lower the preacher without fouling their Sunday suits. Reverend Wilson sat stiffly in his wheel chair looking pensive and worried. Luckily, all survived the ordeal.

When the same party returned after the Sunday service and a typical heavy lunch they found two carpenters packing their belongings and a brand new wheel chair ramp completed. It had been built to city and county code, and the permit was neatly tacked to the apartment door. Reverend Wilson was thrilled but was not as happy as the other senior citizens who no longer had to lift him up the stairs. There were smiles all around.

The older carpenter was wearing a felt hat with a turned down brim, faded blue jeans, an old sweat shirt and had the lean look of a man who stayed in decent shape for his sixtyish years. The apprentice, or perhaps it was the carpenter's grandson, must not have been

SILENT KNIGHT

more than seventeen. He wore a similar outfit as his elder but had a simple white lapel pin on his sweater that bore a red cross. The apprentice advised the group that a gentleman had left a note in the mailbox for Reverend Wilson.

"That is mighty fine work you two have done. I am most fortunate. God is good to me."

Cordial words were exchanged and the two carpenters departed.

As the senior citizens and Brother Wilson reached the apartment, Brother Isaac checked the mailbox. Indeed, there he found a plain envelope addressed to Reverend Wilson.

"Do you want me to open this here note, Reverend?"

"Please do, my friend."

Brother Isaac opened the envelope and saw a card with a colorful crest on the front and SILENT KNIGHT written below it.

"This looks official to me, Reverend; I think you are being invited somewhere."

Isaac opened the card and read, "It says here, "Not unto us, O Lord, not unto us, but to Thy Name give glory."

Reverend Wilson said, "That is a scriptural quote... Psalm 115. What else does it say?"

"There is a hand printed note that says, "Well done faithful servant. May you enjoy better mobility with the ramp.""

"The ramp is a gift. Is the card signed?"

"No, Reverend, it isn't."

"Gentlemen, this is charity. I am not used

SILENT KNIGHT

to being the recipient of such things. I don't know what to say."

He sat at the top of the ramp looking down at the work. His gray hair and wrinkled face looked studious. Soon his mouth spread into an appreciative grin. The eyes sparkled and he looked at his friends and said, "Praise the Lord in all things... a thoughtful act of kindness."

The group passed the card around examining it and word swiftly traveled through the neighborhood that a Silent Knight had been at work for Reverend Wilson.

As the carpenters drove away from the Reverend's apartment, Squire John was smiling. He enjoyed driving the flat bed truck. It was on loan from the local lumber- yard. They had picked it up Saturday afternoon already loaded. Sir Donald seemed to have friends everywhere, and everyone that the Squire had met seemed to exude a sense of personal satisfaction and kindness. As John down-shifted to slow the vehicle, he decided it was time to satisfy some of his curiosities.

"Sir Donald, how did you find out about this preacher?"

The Colonel looked smugly at his Squire, as though he was about to explain some special magic trick he had performed. John could tell the Knight was proud of this mission.

"Last month, I attended a conference at the First Baptist Church. It was attended by clergy and church leaders from all over the State. Reverend Wilson had been asked to give the

SILENT KNIGHT

opening prayer. His prayer was so beautiful and his character so strong that I became interested in learning more about him. I overheard him say that he wasn't able to get out much because of the difficulty he had getting down the steps of his apartment. When I discovered where he lived and spoke to a couple of retired officers that attend his church, we measured the steps and had everything cut to size. It certainly made our job easier. The lumber was donated by another Silent Knight and the millwork was performed by Father Riley - your family priest. You know he makes his own furniture; this was a simple job for him. He volunteered."

"So, you don't provide everything yourself?"

"No. Frequently, knowing the right people and letting them use their talent to meet a need is far better. Not only do you and I feel great about this, Father Riley, Mr. Ramsey, the lumberyard owner and another Knight got a blessing."

"Will I ever meet any other Knights?"

"Yes, Squire. I would like for you to accompany me to the next investiture... if you want to go? You could meet some other Knights and some Squires. It will be on a Saturday... have to give up a part of your weekend."

John was paying attention to his driving but his face showed he was thinking more about the conversation and had more questions.

"What's on your mind, John?"

"What is an investiture?"

"It is a special church ceremony for the Order. Mine was conducted in New Orleans in a beautiful cathedral in Jackson Square... in the heart of the French Quarter. It is an impressive event where our new members are Knighted."

"Like with a sword!? Like in the stories of King Arthur or the Crusades?"

"Very much like that. In fact, some of our members are convinced they can prove our lineage back to 1118... to the time of the Crusades."

"Can the Order prove it?"

"Some say yes, others say no. Personally, I would prefer to focus on the here and now and use the past as a moral compass to give us direction. I don't think anyone will ever be able to prove with absolute certainty the lineage is unbroken."

"Sir, I guess the important thing is... making a difference for people now."

"Exactly! That is a very good way to look at it. That is the overarching intent of the Order and what we pledge, to God, to do in the investiture."

John had stopped at a traffic light and was having difficulty getting the truck back into gear. The grinding noise embarrassed him.

"Squire, it is a standard "H", first is at the top left."

"I know... just can't seem to hit the mark."

"Clutch might slip a little. You are doing fine."

The light changed and the truck lurched

SILENT KNIGHT

twice and finally moved out.

"Is it in secret?"

"Is what in secret?"

"The investiture."

"No, our church services are open to the public. Anyone can attend. We pledge ourselves to God and our country; no reason to hide that. I only wish there were more of us. If we had more chivalry, the world would be a better place."

"I would like to see an investiture, Sir. I know my parents won't mind. I hope it's all right that I told them about the missions you have assigned to me. They are very pleased I am your Squire."

"There is nothing we will do that you can't tell your parents, but remember the idea is anonymity with everyone else."

"Right. I won't tell anyone else."

"If you really want to attend an investiture, consider yourself invited. Your parents are welcome to attend also."

John smiled again as he looked at the Colonel, "Thank you. How did you become a Knight?"

"When I was in the Army, I was a Battalion Commander for an officer who was already a Knight. I didn't know it at the time. He got out of the Army a few years later and invited Helena and me to attend a party. He had recommended us to the Order for Knighthood. We were introduced to several other Knights that evening. It turned out to be an informal interview. Later we were invited to join. Once we were provided the literature and vision of the Order, we were hooked."

"Do you have to be a soldier?"

"No, Squire. As a matter of fact, the Order's only requirements are being a Christian, a professional in your chosen field, and that you live a chivalrous life."

"What does chivalrous mean?"

"I believe it means to embrace a belief that each of us should provide for the weak, sick, elderly, and poor as best we can. To strive to be... gallant and polite. To be a man of spirit, honesty and mettle. I think we must exhibit personal courage in our convictions and treat people with respect and dignity. There are so many people who believe chivalry is dead in our society, it is nice to be a part of something that is trying to bring it back. Random acts of charity can make a difference... one person at a time. Kindness promotes more kindness. Hate just leads to more suffering."

"Someday, can I be a Knight?"

"I think so, John. Otherwise, you would not have been recommended to be my Squire."

John thought about that a moment and smiled.

SILENT KNIGHT

SILENT KNIGHT

CHAPTER 5

San Antonio, Texas, has a beautiful downtown river walk near the Alamo, a sacred monument to Texas independence. The Petersons were enjoying a brief vacation to celebrate their twenty-fifth wedding anniversary. Their hotel overlooked the emerald green Guadalupe River and from their balcony they could hear the festive sounds of the city. Many of the outdoor cafes were still open, taking full advantage of the last days of fall. The temperature on the river was cool, but the atmosphere was warm and delicious. Live Mexican bands filled the air with rhythmic songs while the smell of spicy food teased the senses; colorful umbrellas, tablecloths and people completed the effect.

Colonel and Mrs. Peterson were seated at a table for two, sipping a full-bodied Merlot. They held hands and sat close enough for the Colonel to wrap his arm around Helena. Observers would think they were newlyweds... or lovers. Their conversation was animated and periodically Helena would laugh loudly at some little secret shared between them.

The Knight looked into the loving eyes of his bride, "I have a secret I would like to share with

SILENT KNIGHT

you."

Helena toyed with him, tossing her head to the side. "You have a secret from me? I thought I knew everything about you." Her smile was radiant.

"I always wanted to be your hero."

She smiled again and laid her chin in her hand, focusing intently on the man she loved. "You are."

"No, you make it too easy. If you could read my mind, you would understand the words I cannot express."

She stroked his face as she leaned closer. "Your thoughts have been shouted through a thousand actions. You are my romantic Knight who would scale the walls of any fortress to rescue me. You were born in the wrong age... and I am the lucky one. I married my knight."

She reached across the table and gently grasped the lapel of his blue blazer pulling his lips to hers. Other patrons would look their direction and smile at the obvious fun the two were having. They seemed totally oblivious to the activity around them. And then, the smoking and loudly sizzling fajita platter arrived, interrupting their romance.

The heavy Mexican waiter was wearing traditional Hispanic attire and carried the tray high above his head. He unfolded the serving stand with a quick motion of his wrist and set the tray down with a flourish. The plates were served and the wine was topped off.

"Senor, will there be anything else?"

SILENT KNIGHT

"No, thank you. I believe we can stuff ourselves without any assistance," the Colonel quipped to the waiter.

The waiter smiled, bowed and departed. The food was wonderful, especially the guacamole salad.

As the Petersons dined, Helena noticed a young honeymooning couple. The young man could not have been more than twenty and his bride appeared to be even younger. He was dressed in his Sunday finest and looked a little out of place among the more relaxed customers. The young bride was wearing a simple black dress that made her look quite alluring. Helena thought they were adorable and pointed them out to Donald. She reached into her purse and produced a Silent Knight card. She wrote a brief note, slipped two twenty dollar bills inside, and sealed the envelope.

"Do you remember being that young?"

Her eyes searched his as though she were searching for some hidden truth.

"No, Helena... I was never that young."

"Yes, you were. I just wish I had known you then."

"I don't know, I think we appreciate each other more today because of the hard times we experienced before we met. I wouldn't change a thing for fear it would ruin what we have now. I love you with all my heart. God blessed and cursed me when we met."

Helena looked shocked, "What is that supposed to mean?"

SILENT KNIGHT

The Colonel turned in his chair to face her. He leaned forward and held both her hands.

"Well... I have been so happy for the last twenty-five years that time has seemed to pass too quickly. Time always dragged when I was unhappy. I fear our time together will be over before I am ready. Helena, I regret that we don't have several lifetimes to share. You have taught me to enjoy life. You gather the good of every moment we are together and give it back to me multiplied."

"Hush, you will make me cry."

"I don't mean to. I want you to be happy."

"I know, you just have this way about you that has always disarmed me. You know I feel the same way about you."

Her eyes welled.

"We have had the best marriage of anyone I have known. I never dreamed there would be a man that could make me this happy. Our time together has been perfect."

"Perfect? Moving eight times with the military. Being separated for a year. Those were tough times. Are you sure you don't have Altzheimers?"

Donald laughed to lighten the moment and leaned back to fully appreciate his bride.

"Yes, I couldn't have done that for anyone else. You made me feel appreciated and a part of your career."

"That wasn't hard. You were my partner and best friend. You worked like a mule... but you never looked like one."

The Colonel winked, squeezed her hand and smiled.

Helena leaned forward, and the two kissed. She pulled back slightly, still looking deep into his eyes and said, "I think we should go back to the hotel."

Donald changed his voice to sound like Rhett Butler.

"Hmmm. Madam, I don't believe your intentions are purely honorable."

Helena picked up the game with her best Scarlet O'Hara impersonation and Southern drawl. Her eyes were intoxicating.

"Not likely, Suh."

"Well, I am an honorable man... and I would hate for you to tarnish my reputation, Miz Scarlet."

"Why, Mr. Butler, I believe I could only improve it."

She cocked her head and batted her eyes. She was adorable.

"Waiter! Check please!!"

The waiter arrived a few moments later with the tab. While Donald fumbled for his wallet and calculated the tip, Helena explained to the waiter that she wanted him to deliver the envelope to the young couple a few tables away. She further requested that he deliver it after their departure.

"Si, Senora."

The bill was paid and Donald and Helena walked out holding hands.

The young couple was finishing their meal

SILENT KNIGHT

when the waiter arrived.

"Excuse me, I was asked to deliver this message to you."

The couple looked puzzled and the young man said, "There must be a mistake, nobody knows us here or what our schedule is."

"Senor, I assure you the card is for you and your lady. Please, take it."

The young man took the envelope and read, "To the attractive couple," hand printed on the outside. The groom turned the envelope around so his bride could read it. She smiled and they both looked around self-consciously. Nobody appeared to be watching.

"Open it."

"OK, give me a second."

He fumbled for his pocketknife, finally pulled it from his pocket, opened the blade, and sliced the top of the envelope. As he extracted the card, he noticed a colorful and impressive crest with SILENT KNIGHT written below it. Two twenty-dollar bills slid onto the table. The couple looked at each other and smiled suspiciously. The card read, "Not unto us, O Lord, not unto us, but to Thy name give glory." and a note was hand printed on the left side. "I pray your love will grow ever stronger. Enjoy your meal."

The young bride said, "That is the sweetest thing that anyone has ever done for me. Is it signed?"

"No. It is anonymous. Somebody was very thoughtful."

SILENT KNIGHT

The new husband summoned the waiter.

"Who can I thank for this?"

"Sir, they did not give their name. They are gone."

The couple looked at each other and the bride said, "I'll put the card in our wedding book, so don't let it get wrinkled."

They talked about this simple act of kindness for the rest of their meal and remembered it the rest of their lives.

SILENT KNIGHT

SILENT KNIGHT

CHAPTER 6

It was the Sunday before Thanksgiving and the weather was cold. The fire in the living room had three logs blazing and Ruprecht was uncommonly well behaved, asleep, sprawled in front of its warmth. His full belly from the Sunday lunch scraps had him in overload. The Petersons and John were sitting at the dining room table huddled around several Silent Knight cards and a hand written list of needy members of the community. At the opposite end of the table were four identical grocery bags, each stuffed with a frozen turkey, aluminum pan, dressing mix, four large sweet potatoes, a large can of green beans, a can of cranberry sauce and a small tub of butter.

"John, you recommended the Pendletons, Ken's family?"

"Yes, Sir."

"Good choice. Anyone else you know that might appreciate a little help?"

"No, Sir. I know several other families that are poor but I am not familiar with their needs. Ken's family is by far the most needy in my school."

"OK. Then the first bag goes to Ken's house. You should try to deliver it when Ken is not at

SILENT KNIGHT

home... otherwise, he will know who delivered his class ring."

"I hadn't thought about that."

"That's all right, if he figured it out, it isn't the end of the world. His family is an excellent choice and he is a fine young man."

The Colonel scribbled a note in the card, put it in the envelope, sealed it and addressed it to "The Pendletons." He handed it to Helena who carefully placed it in a grocery bag.

"The second bag, Helena... who have you selected?"

"Mr. and Mrs. Samuels. They are new members of our church. He has been laid off work due to a back injury and will be unable to return till next month. It has been very hard on them. They have two children, about three and five years old. Mrs. Samuels is taking in laundry and babysitting to help make ends meet."

"Another good choice."

The Colonel handed the card to his bride. She wrote a note, sealed and addressed the envelope and again, carefully placed it in another bag.

The Colonel turned to Helena and asked if she had another recommendation.

Helena looked thoughtfully at her Knight.

"You know, Putzi, the elementary school is providing some meals for the homeless. We could send a bag to that effort."

"What do you think, Squire?"

"It is a good... chivalrous cause."

The Knight smiled proudly at his Squire, "I

like it; you are learning fast. So be it."

The Colonel jotted another note and addressed the envelope.

"The final bag is mine. I would like to send it to Ed Smith and his wife. She is suffering from cancer and her daughter and granddaughter have flown in from Georgia to be with her. The family is "tapped out" from the cost of treatment. They belong to the Presbyterian Church and were faithful leaders for years. They used to volunteer frequently and take care of the sick."

"Good choice, Sir."

Helena nodded approval.

"Thank you, Squire. This completes our mission list. There are so many more that could use some encouragement. Sometimes choosing the ones to receive is the hardest part. Let's get on with it."

They loaded the Squire's car with three bags neatly arrayed across the back seat.

When they had finished, the Colonel handed John another five-dollar bill and started to say something but John interrupted.

"I know, it's for the fuel... not an option. What about the fourth bag?"

"Helena and I will deliver it to the school tomorrow. That should be easy, they have a box for donations."

John took the bill and pushed it into the pocket of his new black pleated-front pants. Today he still wore his "church clothes," a bright yellow tie with a colorful design, white

SILENT KNIGHT

button-down collared shirt, and a bomber jacket. The lapel pin was proudly fixed to the leather collar.

"Very good, Squire. Be careful. If you have to, leave the groceries where they will be found easily. In this cold weather, nothing will spoil."

"Yes, Sir."

"Would it be all right if I ask my girl friend to join me for the deliveries?"

"Yes... but..."

"I know, I won't tell her who is doing the giving."

"Right."

"Who is the lucky young lady?"

"Patti Filmore."

"Oh, I know her parents." Said Helena. "She is a beautiful young lady. You must be quite a catch."

John turned bright red.

"No, ma'am... she is the catch."

With that, John winked and drove away.

The Colonel smiled, looked at his bride and said, "I think John is becoming a lot more confident these days." She took his arm and they walked back into the house.

John's first action was to drive to Patti's house. It was a two-story, 1890's vintage home that had seen better days. It needed some paint and leveling but it was still a grand house. Patti's father worked for the telephone company and made a comfortable living. Patti saw John's car, a 1980 Jeep Wagoneer, pull into the driveway and she immediately came out-

SILENT KNIGHT

side. She still wore her Sunday dress and coat. John opened her door and she slid onto the old leather seat and kissed John tenderly on the cheek.

"Where are we going and what is in the bags?"

John explained he had some volunteer work to do and asked if she would like to come along?

"Of course I would like to go."

"Great! You can navigate while I drive. Here's the map."

John helped her orient the map and then checked the address for the Pendletons.

Between the two, they found the house; it was located in a rural area just outside the city limits. At the end of the driveway was a mailbox with "Pendleton" hand painted on the side. As they rolled up the dirt driveway, the house came into view through the tangle of trees and brush that separated the property from the highway. The house was actually a large house trailer that looked as if it were a hundred years old... although that was impossible. John checked to see if anyone was home. There was no car or sign of anyone. When he knocked on the door, a woman with deep dark circles under her eyes answered. She could not have been more than forty years old but it was obvious all forty had been tough years. She had a face that spoke of years of sadness.

"What do you want, sir?"

John was not accustomed to being called "sir." He liked it... and attributed it to the fact

SILENT KNIGHT

he was still wearing his tie.

"Ma'am, I was asked to deliver these groceries to you. You are Mrs. Pendleton?"

"Yes, I am. What is the catch?"

"No catch, ma'am... just groceries."

"Is there a charge?"

"No ma'am. No charge."

"Free?"

"Yes, ma'am. Where would you like them?"

John thought, this is like the delivery to Mrs. Robertson's. I can't get stuck cleaning this house... not with Patti in the car.

Mrs. Pendleton studied John carefully. She looked at the Jeep and saw that a girl was waiting. The car was still idling and after her quick mental review of the situation, she decided that it must be OK. She opened the screen door and invited John in. Once inside, the house was surprisingly clean. Polished in fact. The smell of pine cleaner was everywhere. The little they had was carefully arranged and many handmade decorations gave the place some homespun charm.

John set the groceries on the kitchen counter and moved back toward the door. Mrs. Pendleton began looking into the bag.

"Oh, my. It's a turkey. We haven't had our own turkey for Thanksgiving in years... and look... sweet potatoes too! Who did this?"

"Ma'am, it is from an Order of Christian Knights that recognized your struggle and wanted to help. There is a card in the bag."

"Well, this is the nicest thing I have had happen to me. Is this the same people that got Ken his senior ring?"

Mrs. Pendleton smiled and it was a beautiful smile that lit up her face. The tiredness seemed to drop away from her eyes.

"Ma'am, I couldn't say."

"Who are you?"

"My name is John. I am just a messenger. I have completed my delivery and I hope that you and your family enjoy Thanksgiving."

John opened the door and started toward the Jeep. Mrs. Pendleton came to the door holding the envelope and waved goodbye.

"Thank you... and if you can, please thank the good folks that done this for us. Ken is so proud of his ring."

Her voice cracked as she spoke and John was glad he was not looking at her.

He could feel Mrs. Pendleton's emotion and that would never do in front of Patti. As he drove away, Mrs. Pendleton was standing outside waving goodbye. When the Jeep had disappeared she opened the card. It was identical to the card that Ken had tacked to the bulletin board in his room, except the hand-written note said, "Good people need help now and then. Have a happy Thanksgiving." The woman smiled, repeated the words "good people," smiled and walked back into her house.

Patti asked, "What is in the bags?"

John told her about the turkeys, potatoes and so on, and that he was a messenger for a Silent Knight.

SILENT KNIGHT

"What do you mean, silent night?"

"He is a member of an Order of Christian Knights that perform random acts of charity for people in their communities. They are called "Silent Knights" because they do not want recognition for themselves."

"Silent Knights, that is neat. I never heard of it. How did you become a messenger?"

"I was recommended by my parish priest, Father Riley."

"Who is the Silent Knight?"

"If I tell you, I would have to kill you." John said with a grin.

"You really can't tell me?"

"No, I have promised not to. I am trusted by my friend and I am his Squire."

"You promised not to tell me?"

"No, I promised not to tell *anyone*. Anonymity is why I am needed."

"Sounds rather mysterious to me... but I like the idea of it." She looked at John and repeated, "Squire? What does that mean?"

Patti was looking at John in a way to which he was not accustomed. She looked at him very similar to the way Mrs. Peterson looked at the Colonel. He liked that very much.

"A Squire is a Knight's apprentice or helper. My job is to perform tasks for my Knight and let him remain anonymous."

"I see. Do you like it?"

"Yes. I didn't think I would, but I really do."

"Why?"

"It brings out the best in me... and I feel good

SILENT KNIGHT

about being me. Does that makes sense? I think, in a small way, we give people hope."

"You are really different from the other boys I have met. You're strong enough to be different... compassionate and kind... instead of being concerned about being a macho brute."

John blushed. He had not thought about it that way. He had wanted her to see him as a macho, tough guy, but that would be an act. In truth to himself, he had a reputation for being shy and quiet. This Squire duty was the most adventurous thing he had ever undertaken. Perhaps that is why he enjoyed it so much.

"John, you're blushing! Did I say something to embarrass you?"

"No... I have never been told I wasn't macho... especially by a girlfriend."

"I didn't mean it like that. I like you this way. You are real, not a put-on. You have a good heart."

"Well, if it makes me attractive to you, I can live with it."

Patti kissed him again and hugged his arm and moved to sit directly beside him. John liked that... a lot!

The next delivery was to the Ed Smith residence. When they parked in the driveway, an African American woman of about twenty came out on the front porch. She was a little on the heavy side and had a sad look in her eyes. She appeared to have been crying.

John pulled a bag out of the back seat, checked the envelope address... it was the

SILENT KNIGHT

Smith's. As he walked up the sidewalk the lady on the porch asked, "What can I do for you? You from the church?"

"No, ma'am. I am delivering some groceries to Mr. and Mrs. Smith."

"We didn't order anything."

"No, ma'am. They are a gift from a Christian Order of Knights."

"I don't understand. Who is doing this?"

"They are people that appreciate what the Smiths have done for the community and want to help in some way."

"That is very kind... please bring the bag in and I will get my grandfather."

The house was old and had an unsettling quality about it. Mrs. Smith was dying and the sadness seemed to permeate everything.

Through the dining room he could see into the kitchen where the lady from the porch was speaking to an elderly gentleman. His hair was snow white and he had a Norman Rockwell quality about his face. His facial wrinkles were mostly made from smiling.

The elderly man came to the living room and said, "Myra tells me you have brought a gift for us."

"Yes, sir. It is for your Thanksgiving. Some Christian friends wanted you to have it for your family."

"That is very thoughtful. Please set it on our table, young man. What is your name?"

"I am John."

"Thank you, John. Would you care to speak

to my wife before you leave?"

John had never visited a dying person before. The thought terrified him but he could not refuse Mr. Smith. What would he say to Mrs. Smith? What do you say to someone that is dying? What if his fear showed?

"Yes, sir... if you think it is appropriate. I would like to meet your wife."

"Emily has been very sick... today has been a little better than the last few days. She is tired and ready for God to take her. It is more difficult for us to let go."

"It is a very difficult time."

"Yes... very difficult."

Mr. Smith's eyes welled up and John's heart filled with empathy for this family. It was obvious that they had endured quite an emotional strain. He followed Mr. Smith into a bedroom that had been adapted to accommodate a hospital bed. Mrs. Smith was sitting with the assistance of several well-arranged pillows. A sheet was pulled up to her waist and her arms were crossed over another pillow, an obvious gift from grandchildren as it had "Get well, MeMaw" sewn on the front, surrounded by multiple colored hearts and flowers. Mrs. Smith was losing her battle. The face of death stared at John through deep eye sockets with dark circles under the eyes, framed in a sea of gray stretched skin and white hair. Her face had the hollows of a skull with thin lips drawn over yellowing teeth. Her gaze was amazingly clear; there was peace in her eyes.

SILENT KNIGHT

"Sweetheart, we have company. This young man has brought our family a Thanksgiving meal."

Mrs. Smith's head moved to look directly at John. He was amazed that someone could look this frail and still move.

"God bless you for your thoughtfulness. What is your name?"

Her voice was a little less frail than she looked, and it must have taken a lot of energy for the effort.

"Ma'am, my name is John. Your pillow would indicate you have several grandchildren."

The words seemed to roll through the lady's consciousness and finally engage as she clutched the pillow with a weary hand. John did not feel it appropriate to attempt to explain that he was only a messenger. This was not the time.

"From what I have been told about you and Mr. Smith, I know your children were raised in a good home. Your work with the Presbyterian Church and the good you did for so many in our community is much appreciated. You are in our thoughts and prayers."

"You are very kind, young man."

"Thank you, ma'am."

Mr. Smith moved to his wife's side and stroked her face with his hand. His voice was gentle as he said, "Emily, I just wanted you to meet this fine boy. Now you rest, Sweetheart."

Emily moved her face to better appreciate

SILENT KNIGHT

the feel of her husband's hand. Her eyes closed and there was no further discussion. John turned and left the room. Mr. Smith did not follow. The love this elderly couple shared was evident... it engulfed his senses. The poignant scene he witnessed would play on his heart and mind for years. A stolen moment shared between two partners dedicated to each other for life... and one of the partners was about to slip away. The strength, sweetness, and courage of the Smiths would never be forgotten. The memory of Mr. Smith stroking his dying wife's face was beautifully framed in his memory. The lump in his throat felt like he had swallowed a softball. He moved to leave the house and Myra escorted him to the door.

"Thank you for dropping by. My grandparents have had precious little company since MeMaw left the hospital. It is hard on the visitors, especially their closest friends. It was good to see a visitor and to know others care."

John swallowed hard and managed to say, "Your grandparents are special. It is good you are with them. I only learned of them today. My heart goes out to you."

Myra walked out onto the porch and shut the door behind them.

"Thank you. I fear God may not wait much longer... and sometimes I pray for him to take her. She has suffered so much."

John felt as if Myra was searching his face for some answer to a deeply troubling question. He realized she was barely coping with

61

SILENT KNIGHT

all the emotions she was experiencing. He wasn't sure what to say.

"I cannot imagine how much sorrow you have dealt with. I have not experienced this kind of loss. My grandparents are younger than most; but I believe I would not want them to suffer, either. I think that is normal, when you love someone."

"I feel guilty about that."

"We should hope someone cares as much for us someday. You are here for them. It is perhaps the most important thing you could do."

Myra looked at John with eyes that were deep dark pools. She smiled and said, "I am glad you came to the house. Thank you for your kindness."

Myra extended her hand and John shook it. He moved quickly to the Jeep and backed down the driveway with Patti sitting at his side. She could tell John was deep in thought. She did not trouble him with small talk. She just held his hand. John was pleased that Patti was quiet; his emotions were strained for several minutes. After they had driven several blocks, John said, "Our last delivery is to the Samuels."

Patti said with a grin, "I cheated, I looked at the address on the remaining card and found it on the map. I will navigate."

John feigned surprise at Patti's prowess with a map. He was pleased to have something other than the Smiths to think about.

"I am impressed. She walks, she talks, she thinks, she can read a map and she looks great!

SILENT KNIGHT

Can she cook and do windows too?"

Patti could tell John was trying to push the last experience aside with a little humor. It was cute... in a philosophical way. She thought how different men are about handling their emotions.

"Don't push your luck, Squire John." Patti winked.

"Thank you for joining me. I know this is kind of boring to sit in the car while I make the deliveries."

"I like what you are doing. I haven't known anyone that volunteered to do these things before. I can't hear what you say to the people, but the way they look at you and the way you focus on them is charming to watch. I can't explain it. Without the words, the expressions on their faces tell the story. It is good... what you are doing is very good. I'm glad I came."

"I agree. The faces and... especially the eyes. I find myself having a feeling of ... bonding... bonding is a good word. I bond with these people in seconds. We have nothing in common and yet within seconds, I can feel an attachment. It had never really happened before. For instance, my first assignment was an elderly lady. When I arrived I couldn't wait to get the delivery over with. By the time I left two hours later, we were friends. I have taken cookies to her since then, and my church has sent her meals because my parents told the Supper Club about her. My Silent Knight's wife has taken a meal to her from their church. Last I heard, she is even playing bridge with ladies from the Supper Club."

"Is your Knight's wife active with the Silent Knight program?"

"Yes, she knows all about it and recommends people for assistance. She is a Dame within the same Christian Order as her husband."

"Is she nice? Does she have a Squire too?"

"She is very nice. I don't think she has a Squire: I never asked. I am not sure if there are Squires for Dames. That is a good question. I'll ask if you are interested..."

John looked at Patti. By the expression on her face he could tell she was really thinking hard about this.

"OK. Please find out if Dames can have their own Squires."

They drove about five miles with Patti directing the course. The Samuels lived in a townhouse in a new residential development. New trees and fresh sod marked the landscape. The afternoon sun was setting, producing beautiful rose colors in the sky.

Patti said, "Look, the angels are baking cookies."

"What?"

"The angels are baking cookies."

"What are you talking about?"

"Haven't you ever heard that when the sky turns red, the angels are baking cookies?"

"No... I never heard about that."

"My grandmother told me that when I was

SILENT KNIGHT

a little girl."

"I'm sure your grandmother knew what she was talking about. What was the Samuel's address?"

"Twenty-four, thirty-one."

"OK. This is it."

John pulled into an available parking place. He grabbed the last bag of groceries, went to the door and rang the bell. There was no answer. He waited a moment and knocked loudly on the doorframe. Nobody appeared to be at home. The fact the mailbox label read "Mr. and Mrs. T. J. Samuels" and children's toys littered the porch was good enough evidence for John. He decided to leave the groceries on the porch. As he was walking back to the car, he thought it might be wise to label the grocery bag with the time and date... just in case the Samuels had been out of town. He wouldn't want them to think the bag had been sitting there for days. He turned back and wrote the information on the bag. When he reached the Jeep, Patti said, "That was quick."

"Nobody home. So I left the bag on the front porch and placed the envelope in the door."

"They can't miss that."

"Nope... I will check it later just to be sure it doesn't sit there all night."

With that, Patti snuggled up to John and the two drove away.

It was only twenty minutes later that a depressed Tom Samuels arrived home. As he

SILENT KNIGHT

parked his car, he noticed an envelope stuffed in his front door. His first reaction was anger. The damn bill collectors had been there. Nobody gives anyone a break anymore. Everybody wants their money now. Kick a man when he is down. Just a little luck, just a little time, that was all he needed. He could carry his own weight and provide for his family. Everything was fine until he got injured. It would be OK financially by the end of next month when he got another pay check, but it was going to be tight till then. It would be a bleak holiday season for his family. The thought further depressed him.

As he approached the front door he realized there was a grocery bag beside the door. He asked himself, why would Mary leave the groceries outside? His agitation was increasing as he snatched the envelope from the door.

He ripped the envelope open and pulled out the card. A twenty-dollar bill fell out of the card and onto the porch. Tom bent over carefully leaning on his cane, picked up the envelope and looked at it carefully, his agitation turning to puzzled curiosity.

He looked at the card; it had a colorful crest on the front with SILENT KNIGHT printed below it. He opened the card and read, "Not unto us, O Lord, not unto us, but to Thy name give glory." and on the facing page was handwritten, "You are a good family enduring a temporary hardship. We recognized your struggle and wanted to help. Please enjoy your Thanks-

SILENT KNIGHT

giving meal. God bless you."

Tom was shocked. He had never received charity before. It was embarrassing. He looked around to see if anyone was watching. Nobody was. He picked up the bag and carried it to his kitchen counter where he unloaded its contents. In spite of his embarrassment, Tom admitted to himself that the items were good, and his family would not have had a turkey for Thanksgiving. About that time, Mary and the children arrived. The boys came running in and saw the food on the counter and were fascinated by the size of the frozen turkey.

"Look what we got, Mary."

"Wow! How did you do that?"

"I didn't."

"What do you mean?"

"Somebody decided we could use it. Here, read the card."

Mary took the card from her husband and sat at the table to read it. When she finished, she said, "This is very kind. Who brought it?"

"I don't know, it was sitting outside our door when I got home. It had a twenty-dollar bill inside. You should use it for the little items we need around the house."

Mary smiled and said, "We are almost out of toilet paper and toothpaste. Whoever did this has great timing."

The kids had lost interest in the turkey and left the kitchen and their parents were now alone. Tom was sitting now and staring at the floor.

"Mary, I feel so guilty about receiving charity. I feel like a loser."

She took his hand and said, "Tom, you are the best man I know. You try harder than anyone I know and you have a good heart. I married you because I believe in you. You aren't a quitter. Just like the card says, this is temporary. You will be back to work soon and then we will be able to help someone else. We have done it before."

Tom looked at his wife, "Thank you for never losing faith in me."

"Mr. Samuels, you may not be the fastest horse in the stable... but you are steady... and true... and you are mine. Your love is like that too. You don't blaze and burn out like so many others. You have a steady fire that is always there for me, and the kids. I love you for that and I'm proud of you. Don't you ever doubt it. Together, we can do anything."

Tom blushed. "You never talked to me like that before."

"You were never this vulnerable before."

"I understand... guess my ego needed some adjustment. Maybe this is God's way of giving me a realignment. Showing me what I have been overlooking. The important stuff... friends, my kids, and especially you. You were the best decision I ever made."

Mary's eyes filled with tears. "That is the nicest compliment I ever had."

CHAPTER 7

The Squire had accomplished several Silent Knight missions prior to Christmas and had enjoyed the Christmas holidays. More groceries, a few gift certificates, and a couple of cash donations had been delivered to families. John enjoyed the deliveries and had met some memorable people. Periodically, he would bump into someone around town that had received a Silent Knight package and they would recognize him. The businessmen around town that John had met through the Petersons treated him with a deference that amazed his friends and parents. It gave him a confidence and a sense of worth that he had never known.

It was now early January and school had not yet resumed. Ice and snow were everywhere and the midday sky was overcast with more snow on the way. He drove to the Petersons listening to the tire chains beat on the icy pavement beneath the Jeep. He parked in front of the house and made his way in.

The Petersons were wearing matching plush navy blue sweaters and looking very comfortable. The smell of fresh baked cookies mingled with the scent of a wood fire. The couple had mugs of hot tea with lemon and were reading

SILENT KNIGHT

by the fire when the Squire arrived. They had not been expecting company. The Colonel met John at the door in his usual jovial way.

"Welcome, Squire. Good of you to drop by. What brings you to the neighbor-hood on such a night?"

The Colonel extended his hand to greet John. The young man firmly gripped it and looked him square in the eye.

"Sir, I wanted to see how you and Mrs. Peterson had fared through the holidays and to thank you both for the Christmas gifts you sent me. I really like the shirt and belt... but the pocket-watch with my name engraved on it is my favorite. It was very thoughtful of you."

"Not at all, John, you are family. We don't know what to get young men these days. It was the most difficult present we shopped for this season. I am glad to know it was satisfactory."

"My parents appreciated the card. They were happy to hear your kind words about me."

"All true. You are a fine young man with a great future ahead of you."

The Squire peered toward the kitchen where Helena was removing a fresh batch of cookies from the oven. He said loud enough for her to hear, "Seems like I arrived at the right moment to sample some of Mrs. Peterson's cookies. Hint, hint!"

"Of course! We need a taste tester to ensure the recipe has not gone bad." Helena joked.

The two men sat in the living room and Helena brought another cup of tea from the

SILENT KNIGHT

kitchen for the Squire. It was accompanied by a plate of warm oatmeal cookies. The three exchanged small talk about the weather, school and holiday happenings.

Ruprecht was very demanding. He wanted to play and thought John's purpose in visiting was for him. The growing pup brought toy after toy to the young man and alternated staring at the toy and John as if to say, "Well... don't you like that toy? Throw it for me! Please, please, please, throw it for me."

Whenever John didn't respond by throwing a toy, Ruprecht would whine and disappear only to return with a different one. It seemed the dog would bring new toys until John had one he wanted to play with.

The dog was a welcome distraction. The Squire felt uneasy about asking for anything; however, he eventually got to the point.

"I wanted to ask you both about a couple of things."

The Colonel had sensed an uneasiness and thought John had something important to talk about but had not wanted to push him. "What's on your mind?"

Sir Donald leaned back in his chair and listened. Helena sat at his feet. Both looked at the Squire with anticipation.

"Mrs. Peterson, do you have a Squire?"

Helena looked at John with curiosity.

"Yes... you are our Squire."

Sir Donald and Helena looked at each other and nodded agreement.

SILENT KNIGHT

"That is not what I mean. Have you ever had your own Squire? A girl, to run errands for you?"

Helena and Donald looked at each other again, the Colonel cocking his head and looking at Helena with a thoughtful glance.

Helena responded, "No. We have never had a Maiden. That is the equivalent title given to young women in the "Silent Knight" program. I am not certain there are enough errands to require more than one Squire or Maiden at a time. Why do you ask?"

"Patti, my girlfriend, has accompanied me on five different deliveries over the last two months. She thinks the program is wonderful and would like to be part of it... if that were possible?"

The Colonel looked at Helena and said, "All of our Squires were recommended by trusted members of the schools or clergy. I am not familiar with Patti, but knowing our Squire, and if he is recommending her, she must be special."

Helena added, "I know Patti's parents. Her father works with the phone company and her mother is a teller at the savings and loan. They attend the Baptist Church where Mr. Filmore is a deacon."

The Petersons looked at each other, each searching for a hint as to the other's feelings about the question. The Colonel finally looked at John and threw his hands up in the international "I don't know" salute.

SILENT KNIGHT

"Helena and I will discuss this tonight and let you know our decision tomorrow. Taking on another Squire or Maiden is a big decision. We have an obligation to you for a year. It is not just a matter of a person's desire to serve. There is more to this than we have explained to you. Our Squires are chosen for their potential for leadership, their moral integrity, honesty and finally... for their own encouragement. The Silent Knight program is as much about mentoring as it is about giving."

"What do you mean?"

"Squire, you must look inside yourself to see who has benefited most: you or the people we have served?"

John looked confused.

"I don't understand, Sir."

The Colonel looked at John and smiled.

"John, do you believe that you are the same young man that came to our door four months ago?"

The Squire sat back and thought about that. He was caught off-guard by the question.

The Colonel prodded, "You see no change in yourself? Are you more confident? More sensitive? More caring?"

John pondered these questions. It was a revelation. It was brilliant. He had been had! He suddenly realized that he was the true target of this Silent Knight. It was funny, he had never thought about it that way.

"I see what you mean. The deliveries I make are not just for the receiver, it is for me, too...

SILENT KNIGHT

the Squire."

"Exactly. You, in fact, are our most important effort. The charity errands that you have performed are a vehicle that allows you to reach deep within yourself and tap feelings that could lay dormant if never awakened. Some of our former Squires were permanently changed in the way they view themselves and their relationship to others. All are now involved, in one way or another, in selfless service to others and the nation. Six are already Knights and mentor their Squires just as they were mentored. Seven have entered the military as officers, three were commissioned through West Point, two through the Reserve Officer Training Corps (ROTC) program at the University where I was commissioned in 1943, Texas A&M, one through ROTC at the Citadel, one from the Naval Academy, and three more have served as enlisted. Two have become preachers and one is a doctor. The rest are involved in local politics, church leadership or education. You see, Squire, you are an important member of the community. You have more potential to make a difference than you realize. Our obligation is to help you realize that potential."

John was blown away by this. It was a great compliment, and yet it put him under pressure to make something of himself. The Petersons believed in him, thought he was worth their investment of time, energy, and friendship. In a sense, there was an accounting coming. His first fear was that he would not live up to the expectations.

"You have already learned how little it takes to make a difference in a person's day, and it takes such little effort to feel the joy of giving. Whether it is money, time, a word of encouragement or sweat, the joy is in the giving. When we give to others, we receive peace and happiness in our heart. Our gift to you is confidence, peace and love. You, on the other hand, have returned our gift multiplied. Your friendship, your trust and our ability to watch your confidence soar is your gift back to us. We need you as badly as you need us, only you didn't know it."

John thought... they need me? He was shaking his head. "I didn't see it coming. It was too simple. How did you need me?"

Helena answered, "Your youth, your energy, your interest, your time... they are all precious to us. You will understand this better as you get older. You make Putzi and me feel younger just to be your friend. Your friendship gives us purpose."

John looked at Helena and he could see it in her eyes. They needed him. In some way he filled a void in their lives, a void that he had never been able to comprehend.

"What if I disappoint you?"

The Colonel was surprised by the question. It held far more meaning to him than the mere words. This was all about respect, love and loyalty.

"Squire, you may fail to achieve some of your

SILENT KNIGHT

dreams. If you don't fail at some, you probably didn't dream tall enough dreams. There is no sin in failing. The sin is in quitting... or not "running the race." We don't have any preconceived expectation for you to be measured against. Be bold in your daily life, be respectful of others and stand for what is good and proper. Whether you are a soldier, preacher, doctor, mechanic or ditch digger, be the best that you can be and be happy in your work. There are challenges in any field of endeavor you choose. We want you prepared to rise above the cynicism and the nagging pull of defeatism that haunts each of our lives. Cynicism and defeatism lead to hopelessness and despair. If you allow this world to convince you it cannot be changed, then you become cynical and powerless. We want you to live an empowered life serving God and your community. You have already made a difference right here in our town. You have nurtured hope in others. That seed is planted in you and it will continue to bear good fruit the rest of your life. You can and will make a difference wherever you go; you will be a leader. The fact that Patti wants to be a part of what you are doing is a reflection of your leadership. Helena and I are proud of you. We are proud to be your friends."

The word "friends" had never been more powerful to John than at that very moment. The Petersons had chosen him to pour their energy into. It had not been earned... it was a gift. Their friendship came with no strings attached. This was unconditional friendship. They were there for him.

The Colonel took a deep thoughtful breath and continued, "John, you allow Helena and me the opportunity to make a difference: a difference in your view of the world, a difference in the way you choose to live your life and how you affect others. If you are more confident and compassionate because of this experience, and you carry that with you long after we are gone, then we have been successful. In a sense, you are our investment in the future. We will not issue a score card." Sir Donald smiled and placed his hand on the Squire's shoulder. "You are already a success."

Helena offered cookies to the men and each took one. They sat and watched the fire for awhile in silence. The Colonel finally spoke, "John, can you and Patti come to the house on Saturday afternoon... say about two?"

"Yes, Sir. We can do that."

The Squire beamed a bright smile. Helena returned it and hugged her Knight.

SILENT KNIGHT

CHAPTER 8

John and Patti arrived at the Peterson home promptly at two o'clock the following Saturday. John was obviously proud of himself and seemed at home. Patti on the other hand was reserved and a little nervous. The Colonel had welcomed them at the door and ushered them into the living room where he took their coats. Helena already had some chips and a warm apple cobbler waiting.

Patti's attention was immediately drawn to the unusual military memorabilia and art. "You have a very interesting home... it is lovely."

"Thank you. Helena and I have surrounded ourselves with our memories. You are welcome to look around if you wish."

John immediately began talking about some of his favorite items and relating some of the stories that Sir Donald had told him. They strolled around the living room with John and the Colonel alternating as tour guides. Helena periodically would answer questions about colors, carpets, serving pieces, decorator touches and the heirlooms from her family assembled amidst the other items. The group wandered around for about fifteen minutes before sitting for refreshments. By then, all were communicating effortlessly and Patti seemed comfortable.

After everyone had a cup of hot chocolate in hand and a healthy serving of cobbler, the Colonel began, "Patti, I spoke to your father yesterday. I explained to him what the Silent Knight program is about, and that you had been recommended to us as a Maiden."

Patti looked at John and smiled. "Yes, Sir."

"Your father is supportive and informed me that you had already been quite taken with this form of charity through your experience with John. Together, you and Helena can do a lot of good."

Helena leaned forward in her chair, "Patti, I must confess, I have never had my own Maiden. Putzi and I spoke about this last night and thought of several ways to use your talents and mine in a meaningful way. Our work will be a little different from what John has been doing; however, this will have its own challenges and rewards."

Patti grinned at the cute name Helena had given the Colonel. She thought they were a neat couple.

"Ma'am, I think what you are doing is beautiful. I am grateful to be part of it and will serve in whatever capacity you think is appropriate. Just so you know, I can bake cookies, cakes and know a few recipes for meals. I am accustomed to helping at home and I am not afraid of hard work."

"Patti, you sound too good to be true. You

can start with our attic." Helena winked, laughed and gently squeezed Patti's arm.

The Colonel reached in his pocket and produced a lapel pin identical to John's and handed it to Helena, "I believe your Maiden is out of uniform."

Helena looked at the pin and smiled at her husband. "You are right. Patti, this would be yours if you truly desire to do some good for others."

Patti looked at the pin now held in the palm of Helena's hand. She had not thought about getting a pin, had not even considered it; but she liked it. "Yes, ma'am. I think we can do a lot of good."

Helena took the pin and fastened it to Patti's sweater. "You are my first Maiden."

The young girl felt the pin and looked Helena in the eyes, "I am honored. Thank you."

John and the Colonel applauded.

Everyone was in good spirits and the afternoon passed with much talk about charitable causes and ways to help others. Patti had several good ideas that Helena captured in a notebook. The two ladies were talking like old friends within a few minutes and their animated conversation led the Colonel and John to share an approving look at each other. John leaned toward his Knight and quipped, "I love it when a plan comes together." The Colonel chuckled at his Squire's obvious pleasure.

Helena arranged for Patti to meet her at home the following Thursday afternoon for

SILENT KNIGHT

their first "random act of charity."

Patti was eager to get her first assignment. She drove straight from school to the Peterson's house. Although it was the first week of school after the holidays, her primary thoughts had revolved around the anticipation of her first Maiden duty.

She wore a comfortable red sweater with black slacks and had the lapel pin prominently displayed on her black ski jacket. Not knowing what she might be asked to do, she had packed an extra pair of blue jeans in her backpack.

Helena had seen Patti arrive in her bright red VW Jetta and waited for her at the door. She was as excited as Patti, and it was apparent in her every gesture. They seated themselves at the dining table where Helena handed Patti a book called *The Princess Bride*. There were three shopping bags on the table.

"What are we going to do? Do you want me to deliver these?"

"We are going to deliver these cookies, crackers and sodas to the Wesleyan Nursing Home. I am going to serve refreshments to the retirees there and you are going to read."

"The whole book?"

The look on Patti's face was priceless. It caused Helena to laugh.

"No, not the whole book... just two chapters today. We will go every Thursday until the book is finished."

This was not what Patti had in mind. She had been to a nursing home before. It was not

SILENT KNIGHT

a comfortable place for a young person to be. She was uncomfortable and Helena could tell.

"Patti, all you have to do is smile, read and look pretty. These people will adore you, and you will do just fine."

Patti looked worried. This was frightening to her and she really didn't want to do this... but how could she back out now? She had made a pledge to serve in whatever capacity Helena had determined appropriate. The anticipation of the unknown was playing havoc with her mind.

Helena smiled at her, patted her hand and said, "Trust me."

The confidence exuded by Helena was comforting, but Patti's reluctance was still evident.

They loaded Helena's Suburban and drove about three miles to the nursing home. As they walked into the building, Helena began speaking to the residents by their first names. Some waved and smiled, others came to her and hugged her. Several followed them into the lobby, but most were having difficulty navigating with their walkers or canes. Patti was doing her very best to look calm and dignified. She had a difficult time overlooking the effects Time had dealt these old people. Many were bent, wrinkled or toothless, but all stared at her as if she were a long-lost relative. The mouths all shared one thing in common, they all grinned when she looked into their eyes.

The building looked spotlessly clean but smelled of mingled colognes, urine and a heavy

SILENT KNIGHT

pine scent. Most of the residents were wearing street clothes, a few were wearing pajamas and robes. Overall, the fashion trend was late 1970. It was interesting to see that some of the men sported ties and a few of the ladies wore pearls. In a haunting way, it was as if these people were clinging to the last vestige of their identity prior to entering the nursing home. The feeling created in Patti was sadly poignant.

Helena was busy setting the refreshment table and speaking with all her friends. Indeed, it seemed she knew everyone and they all spoke to her, hugged her or kissed her hand. It was an awesome display of appreciation that touched Patti's heart. Helena was swarmed as she took a moment to look each person in the face and speak to them. Her gift was a smile, a kind word, a hug or a touch. Helena's every move was worthy of a mime. Her body language spoke volumes. It was an overwhelming form of poetic compassion. Patti could not hear the words that passed between Helena and her friends, but it had the power of individual, focused attention. When Helena directed her gaze on these elderly men and women, it was like a spotlight illuminating each one. It was magic to watch and lovely to the senses. Patti wondered if she would ever possess that kind of grace and beauty? Not outer beauty... but the kind that springs from a person's inner self.

"Friends, I have brought you a special gift today. My friend, Patti, is going to read you a story. We will read two chapters today and each

SILENT KNIGHT

Thursday afternoon until we finish it. So, I am going to ask Patti to inform the nurse's desk to announce that the reading will begin in ten minutes so that anyone that wishes to come may have a chance to get here."

With that Patti departed the parlor and found her way to the nurse's desk. She explained that she was with Mrs. Peterson and what they were about to do. The nurse looked at her with a radiant smile and said, "They will be so pleased." Moments later, the public address system announced, "Ladies and gentlemen, the Wesleyan is pleased to inform you that Miss Patti Filmore and Mrs. Helena Peterson are in the parlor serving refreshments. A reading will begin in ten minutes. All are welcome."

To Patti's astonishment, the parlor filled with elderly people, and room had to be made to navigate through the wheel chairs parked in the large doorways that separated the lobby and the parlor areas. It was closer to twenty minutes before everyone was settled enough to begin the reading. At first, Patti was very nervous, but that stopped rather quickly because Mr. Kinchloe was talking very loudly and causing a great deal of embarrassment to Patti as he kept on about how pretty she was. Several of the residents sitting around him would agree and there was general agreement all around the room that Patti was beautiful. Comments echoed around the room about how she reminded this one or that one of their niece,

SILENT KNIGHT

daughter, or granddaughter.

Patti was seated in the middle of the room. As she looked around, there must have been fifty elderly people gathered. They looked at her with anticipation. She began, "The book we have selected for reading is called, "The Princess Bride"..."

Helena asked Patti to speak up, and reminded her that some could not hear as well as others.

She tested her voice level by asking if everyone could hear? Once she had found the right level, she began again, "THE BOOK WE HAVE SELECTED FOR READING IS..."

A hush fell over the room, Patti could hear her own heart beating. At first, she read with very little emotion but as she got into the pace of the book and saw how intently the audience was listening she began to entertain them with a more lively reading. The residents laughed at some lines, some asked to have parts repeated and others fell asleep. A little lady with cottony white hair and a grandmotherly face seated next to her gently held her arm and stroked Patti's forearm. The woman's palsy shook in her hands. It was distracting but Patti would never offend this little woman. She thought it was sweet.

In the back of the parlor, Helena sat on a small couch next to a very feeble old woman and hugged her as she cried quietly. The woman suffered from Alzheimers and apparently believed Helena was her daughter. Helena comforted her during the reading.

By the end of the second chapter, at least ten percent of Patti's audience was asleep. The rest were deeply appreciative and applauded her loudly. Helena had sat back and watched her Maiden bloom. She started as a shrinking violet and ended like a seasoned stage performer. Patti stood up and curtsied. The audience loved her. She even got a couple of whistles. Several staff members had joined the group and were also applauding.

The elderly lady that had stroked Patti's arm tapped her on the side and motioned for her to bend down so she could speak to her. The old hand was soft and wrinkled and shook in a delicate tremor, almost rhythmic. She said in a sweet airy whisper, "Thank you."

At that moment, Patti lost it. Tears welled up in her eyes and ran down her face. One landed on the old woman's cheek.

Without missing a beat, the old woman handed Patti a tissue and said, "Thank you for caring about us."

Patti dabbed her eyes, fumbled for words and choked out, "My pleasure." She squeezed the old lady's hand, turned and moved to Helena.

"As Putzi says, you will do. I am very proud of you!" Helena captured her in her arms and held her tight.

Patti thought, this is the strangest feeling I have ever had. This is so sad and yet so beautiful... it is more than a person can bear. "How do you do this, Helena?"

"I have been coming here for two years. The first time was very hard, but they give me more than I could ever give them. It is a mystery; we came to give, but we end up with the blessing. Few things make me feel as good as serving these wonderful people. Many are lonely, scared or in pain. All they need is a kind word from someone. I am not special, I am just here."

Patti looked at Helena, "I have only just met you, but you are wrong. You don't realize how special you truly are. I don't know anyone that cares for people like you do. You have a gift and you give it to everyone. You seem to make everyone feel like they are important."

Helena looked into Patti's eyes and said, "They are, Patti. They really are."

SILENT KNIGHT

CHAPTER 9

Father Riley stood in the kitchen of the Peterson's home looking quite out of place. Outfitted in his black suit and white collar, he was holding a struggling golden retriever puppy while the Colonel was trying to attach a red ribbon to the dog's collar.

Ruprecht, now nearly full grown, was animated about his displeasure. The dog paced and whined at this young interloper.

John had just entered the room with Helena and both were struck with the humor of the situation. Father Riley's chubby red face seemed to get redder by the minute.

Helena said, "This looks like a job for a woman. You two seem ill prepared to handle this delicate procedure."

She moved between the two men and quickly unsnapped the collar and took the bow from Donald. Father Riley looked at Helena and said sheepishly, "Well... anyone could have done it that way."

John and the Colonel looked at each other and laughed.

Helena had the bow affixed in seconds and replaced it on the pup. "There, he is beautiful. It only took a woman's touch."

SILENT KNIGHT

The Knight turned to John, "You have another special assignment. If you haven't guessed, this puppy is about to get a new home."

Ruprecht moaned loudly and drew the attention of the entire room.

Father Riley walked to Ruprecht and patted him on the head. "It's OK, my friend, that pup will be gone and you won't have to share the Petersons any longer."

John smiled and stroked the puppy while Father Riley held him. "This task already sounds like fun. He is a very cute pup. Does he have a name?"

Father Riley replied, "Yes, his name is Felix."

The Colonel put his arm around the Squire and both stroked the pup. "You are going to deliver this fine animal to a young man that desperately needs him."

John looked knowingly at his Knight. "What is the rest of the story? How do you desperately need a dog?"

Donald had a grin that revealed he was hiding some piece of knowledge from the Squire. "John, the love of a puppy is more important to some than to others. You will deliver this package to Jason Keelor. He is a special case. You will know him when you see him. His dog passed away several months ago and his parents have not been able to replace him. The dog was very special to this young man."

"Where do they live?"

"There is a farm about twenty miles from

SILENT KNIGHT

here. You will take Highway 84 North, and look for a mailbox with Keelor written in big letters on the pole. It will be on the right side. The house sits about one hundred yards off the road. It is a white wood frame house with green shutters with a small barn behind it. You will deliver the pup to Jason or his parents."

The young man nodded understanding and took the puppy in his arms. As he stroked the young pup, he noticed that the dog had soiled Father Riley's coat. He didn't mention it, but smiled knowing the priest would figure it out soon enough.

As he departed the Peterson's he could hear the priest asking Helena, "I think this Puppy soiled me. What do you think?"

John snickered as he walked to his Jeep.

Fourteen-year-old Jason Keelor stood in the bright winter sunlight feeling the warmth absorbed by his black and tan nylon sports jacket. The cold air caused his breath to create a cloud of frost as he rocked from left foot to right, back and forth over the small wooden cross and fresh earth where his best friend was buried only a month ago. His jeans were too long and the cuffs were frayed from constantly dragging the ground. From a distance he appeared to be a short, stubby fellow topped with a disheveled mop of brown hair. In his right hand, Jason clutched some dried flowers he intended to place on the grave. Old age had claimed Hans, the golden retriever. He had been Jason's con-

SILENT KNIGHT

stant companion for twelve years and had loved the boy unconditionally. Visiting the grave had become part of the boy's daily schedule.

Jason would never understand loss. He would be unable to communicate the deep hurt he felt. Throughout his life no harm had ever come to him and no grief had visited his door. Life for Jason was what most of us would consider a monotonous ritual of daily events. Jason Keelor was mentally retarded. His world was different from ours. Money was a foreign concept and death was a mystery this Down's Syndrome child could not comprehend. The one thing Jason truly understood was love.

David and Barbara Keelor were foster parents who had adopted Jason twelve years ago. Two childhood sweethearts who had tried to make a dream come true. David taught school and worked their modest farm. He barely earned enough to cover routine expenses. Barbara mostly looked after Jason. The Keelors were good, church-going people whom life had thrown a curve. Rather than complain about it, they decided to help others. It was good therapy and they had made a difference in their community.

The couple stood at their kitchen window and looked out on the lonely figure of their boy silhouetted in the late afternoon sun. The view was made more desolate by the background expanse of harvested cornfields and barren trees that defined the fence lines.

SILENT KNIGHT

David, on separate occasions, had brought two dogs home to Jason, but neither one would do. Jason was absolutely not going to be satisfied with anything less than an identical dog to Hans. Only those who have worked with special children could know how demanding and defiant they can be. David was torn between purchasing another golden retriever, a cost he could ill afford on his meager teacher's salary, or purchasing the new tires for his old truck. A truck he needed for farm chores and commuting to his teaching position.

Barbara understood the financial situation and had offered to take a job in day care to make the difference; however, Jason was too old for day care and simply could not be left unattended. The couple shared the knowledge that Jason had been their only life-long commitment as parents. Having suffered the inability to have children of their own, they opted to provide a home to children who needed love. Over the years they had been foster parents to over twenty children. Jason was the only retarded child they had fostered, but he had made a home in their heart. The decision to adopt was made with much prayer and soul searching. It had been a good one.

Jason had brought the Keelors more joy than they ever could have imagined. Down's children love and live with abandon. The love is pure and remains childlike throughout their lives. Jason had the reasoning of a six-year-old and would remain there permanently. Perhaps six is the best age to be "frozen." In a strange way, it is a gift. To never lose your curiosity or your ability to cry or laugh when it would be deemed inappropriate by "normal" people is truly a blessing. How often over the course of the years had the Keelors wished they could express themselves as honestly or as freely.

Taking Jason to a movie was a real adventure. He cried shamelessly, cheered or laughed uproariously, depending on the circumstances. Not once in all the movie trips had anyone scolded or chastened them for Jason's behavior. In fact, in their small community, Jason had become a local celebrity as a movie goer. The line outside of the theater during the matinees would see Jason arrive and applaud. Jason, upon hearing the applause, would stop and stiffly bow to the crowd. The crowd loved it and everyone knew Jason by name. It seemed that this boy's movie critique was part of the experience the locals looked forward to. A movie that failed to get a major reaction from Jason was just not worth seeing.

Jason was simple in his life. He believed in God, and believed God protected him. The Bible says that you must believe as a child, without a doubt, and Jason believed. His simple prayers were remarkable in their truth, something that was never lost on the Keelors. During his nightly prayers he would thank God for his parents, grandparents, Hans, a new barn animal, or butterfly or whatever exciting discovery he had made that day. Ever since

SILENT KNIGHT

Hans's death, he had prayed for the retriever's return and was confounded by the silence of God.

As Jason stood alone in the backyard rocking back and forth, an old Jeep Wagoneer pulled into the driveway. The crunching noise of tires on gravel surprised Jason and he turned to watch it approach. The vehicle stopped a few yards away, but the reflection of the sun off the windows prevented any vision of who might have arrived. Jason held his hand over his eyes for shade. When the driver's door opened, a young man exited the vehicle and approached Jason. The stranger wore a nice red ski jacket, blue jeans and a dark Navy blue knit ski hat. He was clutching something inside his coat.

"Hello, my name is John. Is your name Jason?"

Jason looked at the stranger with a comical inquisitive look and cocked his head to one side before responding, "Yes, sir. That would be me."

John smiled at the curious accent and the response. He could tell Jason had no idea what was about to happen. This would be fun.

He handed Jason an envelope and said, "Jason, this is for your parents. Can you make sure they get this? It is very important."

Jason visibly rose to the challenge of pleasing this stranger. He had a mission and his whole character seemed to change faced with this new task. He responded, "Yes, sir. I can do that."

SILENT KNIGHT

Jason turned to go toward the house but the stranger stopped him.

"Not so fast, Jason. I have something else for you."

Confused by the additional information, he turned and asked, "What would that be?"

"It is a friend of mine who needs a home. His name is Felix and he is very young and a little frightened. The home he needs has got to have a person capable of caring for him."

The stranger reached into his jacket and withdrew an eight-week-old Golden Retriever puppy with a red ribbon attached to his collar. The puppy squirmed and whined as it left the comfort of the jacket and was moved into the cold air.

Jason's eyes bulged as he saw this new critter emerge from the stranger's jacket. It was the cutest puppy Jason had ever seen. It looked like a miniature Hans, but more fluffy, more like a small, blonde fur ball. Jason dropped the dried flowers, crushed the envelop into his pocket and walked toward the stranger with outstretched hands. The puppy was soon cuddled in Jason's arms, licking his face, much to Jason's delight.

John watched the boy move toward the house and could see Mrs. Keelor standing at the backdoor of the house. She was probably wondering who was talking to Jason. John waved to her and she waved back. He proceeded to his Jeep and drove away.

Mrs. Keelor watched the Jeep as it moved

SILENT KNIGHT

toward the highway. She wasn't sure what had transpired but it was obvious a puppy was included in the deal. Jason had reached the back door and was standing there grinning from ear to ear.

"Look, Mom. It's a little Hans. Except his name is Felix."

"Who gave him to you?"

"Mister John."

"Who is Mister John?"

Jason looked up from the puppy and looked incredulously at his mother. "I just told you, Mom. Mister John is the man who gave me Felix."

David arrived at the back door and asked, "What have you got there, son?"

Jason looked up with the eyes and smile of an angel and cooed, "It's a new puppy, Dad, and he looks just like Hans."

They gathered Jason and Felix into the house and closed the door. Once gathered around the kitchen table, Jason remembered the note he was to give his parents. He reached into his jacket pocket and withdrew a crumpled envelope. "Mister John said to give this to you."

"Thanks, Jason." David took the crumpled envelope and broke the seal.

Barbara inquired, "What does it say?"

David said, "It says, "Silent Knight" on the front and "Not unto us, O'Lord, not unto us, but to Thy name give glory."

Barbara responded, "That's Psalm 115."

"Yes, that is written here, too."

SILENT KNIGHT

"Anything else?"

"Yes, a brief note that says, "Kindness brings kindness. Please accept this gift as an expression of respect for your devotion to others."

The couple looked at each other and said simultaneously, "It's not signed."

They laughed, hugged Jason and each other.

David said, "Whoever did this has a wonderful heart and a great sense of timing. Gift accepted."

Jason paid no attention to the adults; he had better things to do.

CHAPTER 10

Winter had passed and Spring was in full bloom. The early afternoon air was crisp, clean and cool in the shadow of the magnificent Washington National Cathedral. The investiture was being conducted there in about an hour. The Petersons had driven to the event the day before, and had attended the business meetings that morning in a local hotel. Their Squire and Maiden were arriving with their parents in time for the services. Sir Donald had invited both families to attend. They were dressed in formal evening attire, which was optional for non-participants in the investiture ceremony. All looked radiant. Patti was the most shocking transformation of the group. Her hair was up, off her bare shoulders and the gown she was wearing accentuated her maturation. It seemed that flowers were not the only thing blooming. John's interest and pride in the young Maiden clinging to his arm was announced by the uncontrollable grin he wore. His tuxedo fit well and John, too, appeared more mature than Sir Donald had imagined.

They met out front of the cathedral precisely one hour before the event, as arranged earlier.

SILENT KNIGHT

Knights and Dames from many Priories were present, and all were wearing formal evening attire with black or white tie. Most of the men wore formal military uniforms from the various Services (Army, Navy, Air Force and Marine Corps). Several gentlemen sported kilts with ornate decorations. A few clergy from different religious denominations were talking with each other in a small huddle; they too were apparently wearing the most formal attire available to their position and title. A Scottish band of drummers and pipers was assembling at the right front of the huge cathedral. It was a marvelous, colorful atmosphere. The tourists visiting the cathedral were taking full advantage of the pageantry. The cameras were clicking and those with video cameras were capturing the event.

Mr. and Mrs. Conrady, the Filmores, John and Patti approached the Cathedral and were met by Sir Donald in his U.S. Army mess dress blue uniform. He looked resplendent in the tailored uniform with white bow tie and bright red artillery lapels. His Knight's Cross with symbol for Knight Commandeur hung beneath his tie and many military awards decorated his uniform. His Knight's cape was slung over his left arm. It was the first time these families had ever seen a formal military uniform. The Conradys and Filmores looked apprehensive as Colonel Peterson walked toward them; however, the warmth of his greeting and compliments he showered on them quickly allayed any discomfort.

Sir Donald escorted the family into the Cathedral where Helena joined them. Helena, too, looked radiant in a bright red satin gown. She was the picture of mature elegance... the Rolls Royce, highly polished. The welcomes and friendly compliments passed between them and soon the group strolled through the massive stone structure. The stained glass windows were perfectly displayed by the afternoon sun while the shadows worked their magic on the pulpits, carvings, statues, and icons. The Knight would introduce a passing member of the Order to the two families and more complimentary words would be exchanged. Several Knights had brought Squires and a few Dames had Maidens in attendance. John and Patti had melted into a group where they were sharing stories of their Silent Knight experiences.

The families were seated in the area for guests and the Petersons started walking back toward the entrance. Squire John helped Sir Donald with his mantle while the Maiden helped her Dame with hers. They posed for pictures together at the great doors of the Cathedral.

"Wow! Sir Donald and Dame Helena, you look great! I have never been to any event like this before. I don't know what to say... it defies description. It is like a royal event."

"Squire, this is patterned on ancient investitures for Crusading Knights. It is one of the largest investitures we have because it is at-

SILENT KNIGHT

tended by many of our international brethren. You and Patti should sit with your parents and watch the event. It is filled with pomp and circumstance, but if you listen to the words, it is a very meaningful and inspirational Christian event. We are pledging ourselves to the service of God. Helena and I must get in line for the procession. You and Patti go have a seat and watch this event unfold."

Patti and John sat with their parents. The sound of drums and bagpipes could be heard in the distance; it signaled the start, and the sound continued to grow louder until it reverberated through the entire Cathedral. The assembled visitors stood and faced the entrance. As the music swirled, the pipe and drum commander, dressed in Scottish kilt with fur hat and baton stepped rigidly down the center aisle in a slow, dignified, military half-step. The unfamiliar sound of bagpipes stirred the soul and conjured ancient thoughts. John could feel the hair standing on the back of his neck. A very special event was taking place.

About ten postulants (persons to be knighted) followed the pipes and drums. The men wore tuxedos while the ladies wore evening dresses, their mantles slung over their left arms. The Knights followed the postulants, each wearing their white mantle with the red cross of Jerusalem over their left breast. The procession lasted about seven minutes to get the several hundred Knights and Dames into the church. The entire congregation remained

SILENT KNIGHT

standing. The band stopped playing; the silence that followed was almost oppressive in its depth. It could not have lasted more than one minute but seemed like five. John found himself totally absorbed in the moment.

The Grand Prior stood at the center aisle where he called for the Grand Sword Bearers. They passed among the brethren and each Knight and Dame was given the opportunity to touch the sword with three fingers of their right hand. It took several minutes for the sword to be carried past each of those present.

John could just barely see Sir Donald as a tall Sword Bearer presented him the hilt of an ancient sword. He gently touched the hilt and the sword moved to Dame Helena. When the sword had been passed to every Knight, it was announced that the convent was open. All took their seats.

The sword bearers returned to their positions and the Grand Prior began to speak. "Our Master is God."

The brethren responded, "We are all Brothers and Sisters."

The Prior spoke again, "Non Nobis Domine Non Nobis."

The brethren responded, "Sed Nomine Tuo Da Gloriam." (Not unto us, O Lord, not unto us, but to Thy Name give glory. Psalm 115)

The Prior gave an opening prayer followed by the reading of the orders of the day.

The Postulants were then asked to rise and were presented to the convent. Before leading the Postulants in the oath of membership, the Grand Prior invited all Knights and Dames to join in the recitation. The oath was read by the Grand Prior and the brethren repeated it verbatim.

> *I,_____ , solemnly swear to abide by all lawful precepts, statutes and regulations of the Priory to which I belong in the future, the Grand Priory of the United States of America and the Grand Mastery of the Sovereign Military Order of the Temple of Jerusalem and to obey all lawful requests and demands made upon me under the provisions and rules of the Order, provided that these requests and demands do not conflict in any way with the laws and the Constitution of the United States of America or of the several states, to support and defend the Order and my brother knights and sister dames, doing nothing harmful or injurious to the welfare of either. I am taking this oath freely and without mental reservations in the full knowledge that violation of this oath will result in my exclusion from the fellowship of the Order, removal of my name from the roster and forfeiture of all rights and privileges. I hereby undertake that I will serve this Order to the best of my ability – so help me God.*

SILENT KNIGHT

John and Patti watched and listened intently to the ceremony. The presentation of the postulants was most interesting. As each one was called forward, they handed their mantle to a Knight and kneeled at the altar where the Grand Prior placed the flat blade of a huge battle sword on each shoulder and the top of their head. As the new Knight was tapped with the sword, the Prior would say either in English, Latin or French, "In the name of God the Father, the Son and the Holy Spirit, I do make you a Knight." While this was done, another Knight would touch the heels of the Postulant's shoes with a set of spurs. The new Knight would rise, the mantle would be placed on his shoulders, the insignia of the Order secured around his neck, and he would move back to his seat while the next postulant was called forward.

The ceremony had a reverence to it that John could only compare with a wedding. He hoped that one day, he would be Knighted in such a ceremony.

The historical tradition of Knighthood was read followed by the reading of Psalm 115, verses 1 through 11. The ceremony lasted about one hour and fifteen minutes with promotions, introduction of guests, and the report of the treasurer.

Before closing the convent, the Grand Prior solemnly asked three times as had been done in the Order for almost 900 years, "Is there any Knight or Dame who wishes to speak a word? Speak now and you shall be heard. Is there any

Knight or Dame who wishes to speak a word? Speak now and you shall be heard. Is there any Knight or Dame who wishes to speak a word? Speak now and you shall be heard." The Prior waited a moment and continued, "Hearing no response, the scripture lesson will now be read."

After the scripture lesson, an offering was taken and the sword was passed to the Knights and Dames exactly as had been done to start the Convent, but this time the newly knighted brethren were included.

The benediction was given by a Bishop who looked and sounded like James Earl Jones. Upon completion, the Grand Prior announced that the convent was closed and the pipes and drums came to life for the recessional to exit.

The Conradys and Filmores were pleased and impressed with the reverence, Christian focus and flare of the investiture. They waited with John and Patti until the recessional had completed exiting the great Cathedral to begin searching for the Petersons. It didn't take long, the Petersons were watching for them as they entered the courtyard.

"Well, my friends, what did you think?" asked the Colonel.

Mr. Fillmore spoke first. "This is the most dazzling service I have ever attended. I wish there were more people focused on Christian and chivalric ideals like this. Where is the media when something good is happening?"

Colonel Peterson responded, "Frankly, the

Order doesn't seek media attention; however, because of this shying from publicity, we sometimes get labeled with inaccurate perceptions. For instance, the white mantles have been represented by some as related to the racism of the KKK, when actually they are white to symbolize innocence and purity. Of course, if you attend one of our services, you discover we have members from all races and members from all Christian religions. Christianity, chivalry and the KKK do not mix except in the most perverted misrepresentation of scripture. In fact, you saw that the Bishop who delivered the benediction was African American... and a member of the Order. One of our Grand Sword Bearers is Hispanic and a veteran of the Vietnam War. It only takes a moment to scan the assembled Knights and Dames to conclude this Order has no racial motivations. Others assume we are Masonic or occult... we are neither. Furthermore, nothing we do is secret. Having our services open to the public is a purifier."

The group stood surveying the crowd of Knights and Dames. The gorgeous Spring day was moving toward a cool evening and the shadows were lengthening in the afternoon light. The colors seemed to deepen around them as the light faded. The families were introduced to numerous passersby. It was a moment that everyone seemed to be savoring.

"This was special. I am pleased you and Helena have chosen John and Patti for this expe-

SILENT KNIGHT

rience," commented Mrs Conrady. "I don't think you can experience something like this without being positively affected. It is good to see so many dedicated to this cause. And God knows, the world could use some Christian chivalry. There is so much violence and hate."

Helena turned to Mrs. Conrady and said, "We hope that all our efforts can make a difference for John's and Patti's futures. It would be good for the next generation to grow up in a world that values good works and chivalry. I believe that only through charity and love can we bring about positive change in our Nation, government and world."

Mrs. Conrady responded, "We say, "in God we trust." But many of our leaders sell their soul for a vote. Then they make laws that are absolutely opposed to God's design. In effect, they're legislating morality inconsistent with God's design. The government should leave the morality issues up to the individual."

Mr. Conrady added, "As long as there is law that precludes any man, woman or child regardless of race or religion, from being beaten, tortured, discriminated against or killed, people need to be able to make their own life decisions and let God sort it out at the final judgement."

Mrs. Fillmore commented, "Christians should be known for our caring and compassion, but stand for individual accountability."

Mr. Conrady agreed. "That is a good point; we should all be able to choose how we wish to live, and if our personal morals conflict with the behavior or views of someone, we should be able to respect that opinion, agree to disagree, live and let live. So many people believe they have to be "in your face" with their agenda. If you don't agree with them, they don't have enough respect for your opinion to not infringe on your right to believe your own way. It seems like every disagreement has to be litigated in court or people have to force their opinion on those who disagree. Morality will never be defined by a court of law. When the rights of anyone are violated, the violator should be held accountable by the law. That is the government's responsibility. Morality is about God's authority."

The Colonel added, "Christ said, "Render to Caesar that which is Caesar's and to God, that which is God's." The trouble is, government has decided to define what is God's."

"Right! I never thought of it that way, but that is exactly right. How do we fix it?" Mr. Fillmore agreed.

Helena responded, "We must elect men and women with character to govern the nation. I hope we have learned that character really does matter. Our form of democratic government is the best in the world and is capable of making corrections if the people demand it. Our vote is our strength."

It was obvious that this discussion was careening into a filibuster. The Colonel checked his watch and held up his hands like a referee calling time out. "Before we get too engrossed in this moral debate, there is a dinner and dance at the Army Navy Club that starts in about half an hour. We must start moving that direction. So, ladies, to the car!"

Warm handshakes and farewells were exchanged as Patti and John followed the Petersons to the parking lot.

Mr. Conrady and Mr. Fillmore turned to their wives and said, "We have a surprise. We thought that it would be a shame to waste being all dressed up, having the kids chaperoned and no place to go...soooooo, we made reservations at Trader Vic's for dinner, and we have box seat tickets to the Kennedy Center for *Cats*.

The two ladies looked at each other, smiled and said simultaneously, "Are these our husbands?"

The two men looked at each other and said, "They obviously haven't seen these cats."

All four laughed as they walked toward their car.

As the Colonel maneuvered the Lincoln through the D.C. traffic, Helena placed her hand on her Knight's shoulder. The Squire and Maiden were in the back seat talking about the investiture. It had been a great day and there was a fun evening ahead.

CHAPTER 11

A week had passed since the investiture. Squire John and the Colonel had taken an early drive into the countryside to find a gardening center and nursery. As they turned the Suburban back into the Colonel's driveway, they were met by Helena and Patti. Everyone was wearing work clothes for gardening. The back of the Suburban was filled with colorful flowering potted plants the men had collected. John and Sir Donald were returning to have lunch with the ladies before continuing their mission for the day. The ladies were impressed by the flowers and stood admiring the acquisitions at the rear doors.

"Wow, these are gorgeous, Sir Donald."

"Thanks, Patti, the Squire and I labored endlessly to produce these gems," joked the Colonel. "I'll bet it took a whole twenty minutes to choose them, fifteen minutes to load them and five minutes to check out." The Colonel turned to Helena and said, "You know the nursery donated all this?"

"No, that is wonderful. What happened?"

"John told the manager we were going to plant them in the atrium at the hospital. He said that he wanted to help us out. I didn't know

SILENT KNIGHT

the flowers were free until we checked out. Turns out, he recently lost his mother to cancer and the two of them would sit in that garden when she felt up to walking."

"That is so thoughtful," smiled Helena.

"Ladies, I hope you have prepared a hearty lunch for your men. We have worked up a powerful hunger. You do know that farming is hard work," joked the Colonel.

Patti responded, "gentlemen, your meal awaits you in the kitchen. Follow me."

The group assembled around the dining room table, held hands and the Colonel offered a short prayer.

"Heavenly Father, please forgive us our sins that You might hear our prayers. Thank You for the many blessings You have given us and the charity of the people You place in our path. Thank You for the opportunity to serve You... and may You use our efforts for Your good. Thank You for John and Patti. We pray for Your protection over us. Bless this food and the gentle hands that prepared it. We ask these things in Jesus' name. Amen."

The group began making their sandwiches from the delicately arranged platters and passed the potato chips around. Soon they were all engaged in discussions about the mission for the day, the investiture and other potential missions.

Sir Donald looked at his Squire and said, " John, it is hard to believe that you have been working with me for nearly eight months now.

SILENT KNIGHT

Soon you will be retired."

John looked like he had been stunned by the comment. "It has gone quickly, Colonel. I had not thought about the year moving by so fast. I must say, I do not look forward to it ending."

"We still have four months, Squire. You have done well. In fact, you have been among the very best. Although your Squire duty will come to an end, our friendship and your access to us will not change. We are committed to you."

The Colonel looked around the table. The expressions on the faces made him wish he had not brought the subject up. The table conversation dropped off. He tried to recover the situation.

"Let's look at it this way, you are two thirds through your Squire duty. What have you learned from this experience?"

The Squire looked at Sir Donald thoughtfully and said, "I have learned that what is most valuable is not what you have in your life, but who you have in your life. That giving really is better than receiving... and that there are far more good people in this world than I had originally thought."

"That is very, very good, John." The Colonel smiled proudly.

"I am not finished... I have learned more," interrupted John. "I have learned that even a young person can make a difference and... that a kind word can be very powerful. It can create hope."

There was silence around the table. Every-

SILENT KNIGHT

one looked at John. He looked puzzled.

"What... what did I say?"

"John, you have just validated everything the Squire program is about." The Colonel smiled broadly and feigned shock. "... and you did it so eloquently."

Patti smiled, "that's my boyfriend!"

Helena got up and hugged John and looked at Sir Donald. "You will do, Squire."

John looked at the Colonel and said, " Sir, may I ask a personal question?"

"Well, I guess it depends on how personal." The Colonel winked. "But... go for it!"

"When we first met, you mentioned one Squire that was not with us anymore. What happened?"

The Colonel looked at his plate. It was the first time the Knight seemed uncomfortable about anything.

"Sir, I apologize for asking..."

"No apology necessary. It is a good memory... but it is sad because of the pain that comes with losing someone you love."

Helena also looked grieved by the question. She remained quiet and appeared to be waiting for the Colonel to tell the story.

The Knight cleared his throat, continued looking at his plate and began, "Anthony Merritt had been recommended to us for Squire duty about fifteen years ago. Tony was tall, blonde, athletic and a leader in school and the Methodist Church. His time with us was every bit as special as our time with you. We

SILENT KNIGHT

talked about many things and he visited us just as you do... because he wanted to. We enjoyed a very special friendship. Tony became like a son to us. After his Squire duty ended, he graduated and continued to stay in touch. He never missed an opportunity to visit us when he could break away from college. We wrote or called each other every week. Frequently, he would pass the name of some needy person to me, and an idea on how to meet that need anonymously."

"One of the families he had been most taken with was the Sheffields. Mr. Sheffield was a very successful builder who was crippled by an accident and could no longer work. The mother was a substitute teacher. They had three small children ranging in age from three to seven. Mr. Sheffield struggled with depression and bounced between menial jobs. Their savings depleted... they were evicted from their own home and were living in a shelter. It took all Mrs. Sheffield's energy to keep the children from being sent to foster homes. These were good people with absolutely no safety net. When we found out about them, three churches came together to provide an apartment. We got a steady job for Mrs. Sheffield and Mr. Sheffield became a substitute teacher himself. Eventually he got his teaching certificate. Tony got the Methodist Church to commit some funds to this family. He was a bold and committed fundraiser."

"The Sheffields were able to stand on their

SILENT KNIGHT

own in about six months, but Tony worried about those children ever getting an opportunity to go to college."

"After Tony graduated from high school, his father was transferred to Ohio, so his visits were less frequent; however, we stayed in very close touch with Tony for the next three years. Suddenly, he stopped calling and the cards stopped. We phoned his parents but there was no answer. After a month of no contact, we got worried and contacted the school, but because we were not relatives they could not help us."

"About two months passed when Tony's dad called to say that Tony had collapsed at school. After numerous tests, it was discovered that he had a brain tumor. He had been in an intensive care unit for several weeks. Emergency surgery had to be performed and Tony had been in a coma for weeks. When he regained consciousness, he asked for us. Of course, we dropped everything and went to him immediately."

"His parents were exhausted and we took turns sitting with him. The surgery had left him paralyzed from the neck down, talking was very difficult and the left side of his face drooped badly. Even his breathing was assisted. The doctor's report was that the tumor was malignant and his case was terminal."

"He was coherent for almost three more weeks before lapsing into another coma. His courage had been inspirational. We were there when he died... quietly. He was on so much life support, we didn't know he was dead. His heart was kept beating, but the brain had stopped functioning."

The Colonel took a deep breath and said, "They turned off the machines and it was over."

Helena wiped the tears from her eyes and sat back in her chair. The silence was a long one.

The Colonel continued, "Tony's last conversation with us was about the Sheffields. He had a fifty thousand dollar life insurance policy. Forty thousand went to his parents and ten thousand went to a college fund for the Sheffield children. Over the last ten years, through good management, it has grown to more than sixty thousand dollars. The oldest child got a full scholarship to West Point this year. Because of Tony's thoughtfulness, all three children will have the opportunity to attend college. His father told me that Tony changed his will a week before he died. Two days later he lapsed into the second coma and never came out. He wanted to have a legacy."

Patti shook her head. "Thank you for sharing Tony's story with us. It seems you made quite an impression on Tony."

Helena looked at Patti and said, "I think Tony made the impression on us. We still marvel at his strength of character."

John asked, "Why does God let things like that happen to good people?"

The Colonel looked at John and responded, "God has a purpose for everything. In His per-

SILENT KNIGHT

fect wisdom, I believe Tony served God's purpose. I often wonder if I was the one that Tony was intended to affect. There are many others that Tony affected; however, I am a better man for knowing Tony. I am more thoughtful, more sensitive, and more appreciative of others because of Tony. If the effect that Tony had on our lives affects you and Patti and those we encounter, then God's will was served by Tony's life and death. Of course, I believe there are far worse things than death, especially for a Christian. But that is for another discussion, perhaps another day."

The Colonel smiled and said, "Tony would like what we are doing today."

With that, the Colonel stood up, signaling the others it was time to do some gardening.

Forty minutes later, the four of them stood in the atrium of the hospital surrounded by the potted plants, a few tools and a small wheelbarrow. They had a good bit of work to do here. The atrium had not been well maintained. Dried leaves had collected in the corners, grass grew in the sidewalk cracks, tangled vines and weeds threatened to overtake old flowerbeds. As the group worked, hospital patients would come to the hallway windows that lined the atrium and peer into the garden. Some pushed breathing machines or I.V. poles around as they strolled. A young couple came into the garden pushing a wheelchair. A bald-headed child with gaunt eyes and wearing a hospital robe sat in the wheelchair; he looked very frail. The couple sat on a bench beside the child to watch the gardening.

Patti raked, John tilled, Helena weeded, and the Colonel pruned. It took nearly an hour to get the sidewalk edged and the flowerbeds prepared to accept the plantings. Helena had trimmed a small rose bud from one of the bushes and had handed it to the child in the wheelchair. The young patient had clutched the flower, looked at Helena and smiled weakly. No words were exchanged, Helena just removed her work glove and stroked the child's face. The young patient looked at the flower and smelled its fragrance. The parents thanked Helena and she returned to her labor.

It had taken about two full hours to transform the atrium into a respectable flower garden. It wasn't plush, but the transformation was impressive. About a dozen patients had moved into the garden and were sitting on the benches enjoying the new view. The Petersons and their charges loaded their tools into the wheelbarrow and John was moving it toward the exit. One of the elderly patients said, "Thank you, you don't know how much this lifts my spirit. God bless you."

Another patient started clapping and soon the atrium was filled with the sound of applause.

SILENT KNIGHT

SILENT KNIGHT

CHAPTER 12

The Senior Prom was two weeks away and Casie Heath was dreading it. She was a lovely girl and popular with the young men... but she had no dress for the Prom. The money she and her brother, Mark, earned bagging groceries at a local grocery store was used to provide food for the family and any other needs. Her mother was divorced, her father was a "deadbeat dad" and the secretary's pay her mother earned barely made the rent and car payments, but between the three of them, they were survivors.

The two dresses that Casie owned hung in her closet like old dish rags. She had worn them so often to church or parties that everyone knew them and recognized her from a distance just by the dress she wore. It was a silent embarrassment to her. She wouldn't mention it to her mother: her mother's wardrobe was not much better.

A young man had invited Casie to the Prom and she had accepted in an excited gasp, long before she thought about the lack of a proper dress. Now, she wished she could back out of the date rather than suffer the embarrassment of wearing either of the dresses in her closet.

Mark, Casie and Mrs. Heath were seated at

SILENT KNIGHT

the kitchen table in their small apartment finishing dinner when the doorbell rang. Mark pulled back from the table and moved to the door. His extra large New York Yankee T-shirt was untucked and made his frame look very lean. His jeans were threadbare at the knees and cuffs, the tennis shoes grass-stained and worn. The appearance of the young man at the door was far different. Mark thought the guy must be lost; however, before he could inquire, the visitor asked. "Does Casie Heath live here?"

Mrs. Heath overheard the visitor's question and asked Casie if she was expecting anyone. Casie responded by shaking her head and looking curiously at her mother. Mark was only gone a moment but returned to the table saying, "Casie, there is a kid at the door asking for you. Must be a new boyfriend. He is really overdoing it."

Casie looked surprised. "Who is it?"

"I don't know. He didn't say and I didn't ask."

Mrs. Heath said, "Casie, don't be gone long. Your dinner will be cold."

Casie rose from the table, checked her appearance in the small mirror by the kitchen door. She smoothed her hair and retied the denim work shirt between her naval and breasts. She approved of the minor corrections and moved through the living room to the front door. She did not recognize the young man standing on the porch in the fading evening light. He wore a navy blue sport coat with a

SILENT KNIGHT

lapel pin in the collar.

As she approached the door, the young stranger said. "You must be Casie Heath."

John thought, she is prettier than I expected.

"Yes... yes, I am."

"I have a card for you. My instructions were to deliver it into your hands. It is from a Christian Order of Knights." The young man reached into his coat pocket and produced a white envelope.

Casie slowly opened the screen door and took the envelope from the polite young man. "I don't understand. What would a Christian Order of Knights have to do with me?"

"I am sure the card will explain everything. My job was to deliver this card to you. My job is done. Have a pleasant evening, Casie."

John smiled and extended his hand to shake hers. She grasped it and said.

"Thank you."

With that, the young stranger departed, and Casie shut the door.

As she walked back to the kitchen, her mother asked, "What was that about?"

"An attractive young man delivered a card to me. He said it was from a Christian Order of Knights." Casie's smile revealed her excitement.

"What? Was he kidding? Is this a joke?" asked Mrs. Heath.

"Well, the envelope is addressed to me... the messenger looked pretty serious, too."

"Open it, Casie! We are going to pass out

SILENT KNIGHT

from the suspense!" teased her brother.

Casie opened the card. On the front was a beautiful crest with SILENT KNIGHT printed under it. When she opened the card another smaller envelope was inside. The card read, "Not unto us, O Lord, not unto us, but to Thy Name give glory. Ps. 115"

On the left facing page was hand written, "Casie, you are a lovely young lady with great integrity and character. We pray you find something nice for the Prom."

Casie handed the card to her mother while she opened the second envelope. As she unfolded the note it read, "GIFT CERTIFICATE" at the top. Below she read, "This certificate entitles Miss Casie Heath to a shopping spree at Casual Fashions for any amount up to $250.00."

Casual Fashions was an upscale dress shop that carried fine clothing. Most of the young women in Casie's school would acquire their prom dresses from this popular establishment. Casie read the certificate twice more before leaping up from the table and dancing around the room. She kept repeating, "I'm going to buy a dress! I'm going to the Prom!"

Her mother snatched the certificate from her hand and read it. She jumped into Casie's arms and joined her in the happy dance. "Casie, I am so thrilled for you."

Mark Heath sat at the table looking at the two crazy women swirling around the room and shook his head. "Does this mean I can have

SILENT KNIGHT

your desert?"

Three blocks away, Ricky Berry sat on the porch of his run down home wishing he were on another planet. Ricky's girl friend, Carol, was expecting him to take her to the Prom. He had no way of dressing for a night like that. He did not even own a suit, much less a tuxedo. His father was an alcoholic and his mother worked as a housemaid. He had three younger brothers and a sister. The money Ricky made mowing lawns was all that kept them from starving. His only hope for an education was a basketball scholarship or the Army. Reverend Tyrone Wilson, the elderly pastor of his African American Church had written letters of recommendation to several Bible colleges in hopes that Ricky might become a preacher using basketball as a means to scholarships in those institutions. Ricky was a good kid with decent grades and had a natural gift as a leader. Unfortunately, what others could see in Ricky, he did not see in himself. As with many people, Ricky was his own worst critic.

Ricky was in the "waiting game" to see how his life was going to move from this life of poverty. He was overwhelmed by his poverty and wondered why God did not help him.

Tomorrow, he would have to tell Carol that he was not going to the Prom. He would make up a story about having to work. He couldn't tell her that he could not afford to rent a tuxedo for the evening.

At that moment, an old navy blue Jeep

SILENT KNIGHT

Wagoneer pulled up in front of his house. The driver's window opened and a young man called him, "Ricky, it's me, John Conrady."

Ricky knew John from school classes they took together. He walked out to the road and said, "John, what are you doing here?"

"I was asked to deliver a message to you. It is from a Christian Order of Knights. You will like it."

"What are you talking about, man? I don't know anything about any Christian Knights."

John handed him the envelope and Ricky stared at his name printed on the front.

"Do you know what this is about, John?"

"Yes, you will like it. I was glad to see this happen for you. I have to go."

John put the Jeep into drive and started raising the window. Ricky thanked him and waved goodbye.

As the Jeep disappeared up the street, Ricky walked back to the light of the porch and opened the card. He stood near the end of the porch reading in the light from the front room window. There was the colorful crest with SILENT KNIGHT printed below it. Ricky thought about this and had heard Reverend Wilson speak of being helped by a Silent Knight. He smiled at the memory of Reverend Wilson's story. He opened the card and read, "Not unto us, O Lord, not unto us, but to Thy Name give glory. Ps. 115". On the facing left page was hand written, "Ricky, you are a role model for your brothers and sister. God loves you. Enjoy the

SILENT KNIGHT

Prom." The card was not signed. Another small envelope inside contained two tickets to the Prom and a gift certificate to Tuxedo World for one free tuxedo rental.

Ricky was stunned, he stared at the certificate and a huge grin spread across his face. He turned, still deeply focused on the card and leaned toward the pillar supporting the porch roof. He missed it completely and fell into the flowerbed. He lay there for almost five minutes laughing at himself and clutching the card. He hoped nobody had seen him.

… SILENT KNIGHT

SILENT KNIGHT

CHAPTER 13

It was a hot and humid July. Summer had arrived in full glory. Temperatures soared into the nineties during the mid-day but would cool to the seventies during the night. Fortunately, the Peterson's home was an oasis of comfort for the assembled dinner guests. The purpose of the evening was to honor John as he completed his "active duty" as a Squire.

The guest list included John's parents, Father Riley (a member of the Order), Patti, the Filmores, and Mr. Ramsey (another member of the Order and the owner of the local lumberyard). It was a coat-and-tie affair and Helena had gone all out. Upon arrival, the guests had been ushered into the living room where elegant platters of hors d'oeuvres were arranged. The shrimp cocktail and oysters on the half shell were going quickly. The Colonel and Father Riley sipped Scotch, the other gentlemen had sherry while the ladies chose between two fuzzy navel punches... one alcohol free and the other spiked.

No doubt, the Petersons had gone all out to make the evening special for their Squire. The dining room table was set for ten. A beautiful white tablecloth with silver candle holders, in-

SILENT KNIGHT

dividual crystal salt and pepper shakers, polished silverware, and the Petersons' best crystal and china adorned the setting. Two wine carafes were placed at each end of the table, one with white wine and one a dark red Merlot. A centerpiece of spring flowers finished the table decor. The Persian carpet colors of burgundy, navy blue and hunter green spun a dark richness to the interior. The lamps were dimmed to accentuate the candle glow, and a few of the military artworks had subtle individual lighting. In all, the house had the aura of a castle chamber.

John and Patti looked fabulous in their dinner attire. The young Squire wore a navy blue blazer with a crisp white shirt and bright yellow tie. His lapel pin was prominently displayed. Patti wore a luminous red sleeveless cocktail dress. Her pin secured a silk scarf draped round her neck. They drank mint, iced tea while mingling with the guests. Both appeared to be far more mature than their age would indicate. Sir Donald smiled as he studied his Squire from a distance. This was not the same young man that arrived at his door a year ago. John was smooth, well groomed, well mannered, and carried himself with an air of confidence. His smile was easy and his heart was good; he radiated a gentleman's charm. The Colonel was proud of John.

Patti was equal to the evening. Her time as Maiden was only half done. She and John had discussed the end of the apprenticeship and viewed this event as John's leap into another stage of life... adulthood. Both looked forward to starting their high school senior year in the fall; however, their view of life and what was important had radically changed. They were followers no more, they set their own course.

At dinner, the Colonel asked Father Riley to say grace. The prayer was long but very eloquent. The prayer was for John and for his empowered future as a role model and leader.

Once the wine was poured, the Colonel proposed a toast, "To my trusted Squire, a noble gentleman, and my very good friend... a man who has made a difference for many, has given Helena and me much more than we could give... and to a happy future... to our friend, John, may we always remain close."

The group responded with, "To Squire John!" Each guest congratulated John in their personal way.

When the group settled, John rose and held his wine glass (filled with mint tea) at waist level. The dinner guests became quiet.

"Sir, I too desire to make a toast." John stood erect and tall. He appeared to gather himself. He wasn't nervous, he was among family.

Everyone silently admired the transformed figure of this young man as he towered over them. All knew the previous year had done much for shaping John Conrady.

"To my second family... to my unexpected teachers... my friends whom I love... to people that care... that make a difference for strang-

SILENT KNIGHT

ers and make a kid like me feel important... to Sir Donald and Dame Helena, thank you for your investment in me."

The group responded, "To the Petersons."

A tear rolled down Helena's face as the others drank the toast. The Colonel beamed with pride.

Dinner was awesome. Helena and the Colonel had prepared everything. A mandarin salad preceded the main course. The garlic and rosemary lamb was accompanied by small red potatoes marinated in crushed capers, lemon juice, parsley, zest of lemon, olive oil, black pepper and anchovies... they were a delicious side dish complementing the robust lamb flavor. A second choice of stuffed smoked salmon was available accompanied by spiced rice, fresh green beans and almonds. For desert, and causing an audible groan from the stuffed diners, was homemade vanilla ice cream with a whiskey and pepper topping.

The conversation was lively, most revolving around John's future direction, college and profession. No decisions were made but lots of opportunities existed.

Patti told a few private stories of embarrassing moments for John as he endeavored to complete his Silent Knight tasks. Most had never been heard and were quite cute. Patti had a gift for telling a story. John laughed at himself and returned a few funny stories in Patti's direction. It was an enjoyable evening.

Mrs. Filmore was enchanting as she spoke

SILENT KNIGHT

about travels her family had made. They particularly enjoyed sailing, which also happened to be a passion of the Petersons. Other common interests were cooking and reading history. Conversation was not lacking in this group.

Father Riley had a remarkable sense of humor and could have sold tickets for a comedy act. He was never at a loss for words. He had stated in very serious tones that his only reason for participating in this Silent Knight program was not out of respect for the program or what it did for the community… it was so he could be invited to the Petersons' dinners. Everyone laughed and mocked agreement with his reasoning.

The Petersons acknowledged the compliments and were obviously pleased by the success of the evening.

Prior to rising from the dinner table, the Colonel reminded both John and Patti, "while your active participation as a Squire or Maiden may come to an end, the friendship and your access to us will never end. You are welcome here. You are family."

Sir Donald reached beside his chair and produced a brightly wrapped box. "To help you remember your time as my Squire, I wish to present you with a small gift that will serve you well for the rest of your life."

The gift was passed to John.

"John, every Knight must have a sword. This is your Light sword."

SILENT KNIGHT

The guests appeared confused. The box was not big enough for a sword.

The Colonel continued, "it is a small study Bible. We are to put on the armor of God and His word is our sword... therefore, I am arming you for life."

John unwrapped the Bible and found it bound in leather, with his name printed in gold on the cover. Inside, the inscription read:

For John,
May God bless you and keep you.
           Love,
           Donald and Helena

John gripped Helena's hand and said to the Petersons, "thank you for making me feel special. I will miss our random acts of charity. You have made a difference in my life that I will never forget. Someday, I hope to join you in the ranks of the Sovereign Military Order of the Temple of Jerusalem as a Silent Knight."

Coffee and brandy were served in the living room. Cigars were offered to the gentlemen. Only Father Riley and the Colonel smoked. The gentlemen retired to the patio where the temperature had cooled in the darkness and a large overhead fan helped circulate the air. The Colonel and Father Riley spoke about all eighteen of the previous Squires. John had met three of them during visits to the Petersons and he relayed a few of their stories. Mr. Filmore and Mr. Conrady were amazed by the closeness of this Christian brotherhood. The comraderie and traditions of the Order were a topic of conversation. It was apparent that the Colonel and Father Riley had a genuine admiration for each other, the kind of friendship that is forged over many years and shared traditions.

Mr. Conrady and Mr. Filmore spoke of the changes that had occurred in the behavior and hearts of their children. Mr. Conrady stated that the stories his son had shared had affected him, also. He now saw opportunities for "random acts of charity" all around him. Mr. Conrady put his arm around his son, turned to the group and said, "I am very proud of him."

The Colonel was very pleased by the conversation with the parents of the Squire and Maiden. The Conradys and Filmores could be invited to join the Order. He would confer with Father Riley and Mr. Ramsey another time to obtain their support for submitting the recommendation as postulants of the Order. From his experience, it was a cinch. He smiled at the thought of both families being knighted. It had indeed been a good year.

The party lasted till the small hours of the morning. Father Riley thanked the hosts and prepared to leave. Everyone followed his lead. All the guests departed together. John thanked the Petersons again for their hospitality as he helped Patti into his Jeep.

As the last car pulled away, the Knight and Dame entered their home and shut the door behind them. Helena took off her shoes and

SILENT KNIGHT

hugged her Knight. "I thought the evening was a huge success. I think John was pleased."

"Your lamb was outstanding," remarked the Colonel.

"The ladies had a lot of fun. Mrs. Filmore didn't realize the fuzzy navel punch was loaded. She had a wonderful time. Kept talking about how good the punch was."

They both laughed.

"Both our charges' mothers are fine people. I enjoyed their company very much. Do you think they could be recommended for acceptance into the Order?"

"What a great idea... wish I had thought of that myself."

The Colonel hugged his bride and grinned a mischievous smile.

CHAPTER 14

Summer had ended and school was back in session. John and Patti were enjoying being seniors. Soon they would have their rings and the football games would be starting. The first scrimmage was planned for Friday. John's tour as a Squire was done; however, he was amazed at the changes in himself. His self-confidence was high, his dress was more mature, his grades were up, and he had influence in the social strata of his peers and other students. He didn't know when it happened, but he had become a leader.

Patti had remained busy with Dame Helena by visiting the nursing home each month. The book *Princess Bride* had been completed and a new one started. The visits were an amazing experience for this young Maiden. Patti realized now what Helena had meant when she said, "they give me so much more than I could possibly give." The ladies and gentlemen of the Wesleyan loved Patti. She found herself visiting the home every week. It was a self-gratifying experience. The more love she poured out, the more love came back. She had embraced her fear of the nursing home and it had evaporated like fog. The old people were lonely and responded to every act of kindness.

The aging process was simply part of life. At its zenith, it is a time to reflect on precious memories. Patti had heard many stories from nursing home residents. Their eyes would come to life as they recalled meeting their wife or husband, or recalled the birth of their children. Many would describe their homes, others would share pictures of grandchildren. All they needed from Patti was an attentive ear. It was so little to give. Patti also understood what Helena meant when she said, "I am not special; I am just here." Anyone with a little time, compassion, selflessness and love could take her place. It was unfortunate that so few were willing to give of themselves. The need was so great.

Patti and John discussed these needs and came up with a plan. It centered around the home economics class at school. Every year, the "home ec" class would learn to cook and prepare complete meals. Salads would be the subject one week, main courses the next, followed by desserts. The meals would be shared by the class, but John and Patti asked themselves, "why not share the meals with the nursing home?" A panel of judges could be identified from the elderly residents and first through third place winners could be declared from the assorted entrees. This would serve several purposes: first, to get some young people into the nursing home to visit with the residents; second, to encourage the youth to visit; third, to give the residents a task or purpose; and finally, to urge the students to compete for a higher grade in "home ec."

The idea received cool initial responses. The teacher, Mrs. Williams, was not a giver, and was less than encouraging when Patti spoke to her about it. John had worked an "end run" with the principal. He asked Mr. Lucas in a casual conversation, if the school had any outreach programs in the community. After a long thoughtful pause, the principal said. "No."

John commented that it was too bad, because the school had recently started values training programs during homeroom. It was just talk with no action.

The following week, John learned that Mr. Lucas had asked all the teachers if they had an outreach program working in any of their classes.

Mrs. Williams, as had been expected, volunteered Patti's idea as her own. Mr. Lucas was pleased with the project and told her to execute it as soon as possible. He further encouraged the other teachers to present ideas at their next meeting.

When John and Patti heard the news they were elated! Patti exclaimed, "Colonel Peterson always said that you didn't have to stand in the spotlight to lead. By asking the right question, at the right time, you can lead from the third row."

John grinned and nodded agreement. "We just proved that concept."

SILENT KNIGHT

Patti phoned Helena and related the story that evening. Helena laughed out loud and praised her Maiden for the inspiration. "Patti, this is delicious! Donald will be so proud of you. He will have to call John. You know, Donald is interviewing a new Squire tomorrow evening. You'll never guess who Mr. Lucas recommended."

"I have no idea."

"Kenneth Pendleton."

"Wow! What a great idea. With a little encouragement, Kenneth could do great things."

"Donald and I are excited about it. He spoke to Mrs. Pendleton yesterday. She was thrilled for Kenneth and thinks the Silent Knight program is awesome. Donald had to tell her, because she asked, that it was standard practice not to talk about random acts of charity like Kenneth's ring, or the Thanksgiving meal, or Kenneth's job at the lumberyard. He would not confirm or deny he knew who the benefactor was. She understands that anonymity is important."

"Helena, I didn't know about the job."

"Neither did I. I guess Mr. Ramsey and Donald teamed up."

"That is so neat. Kenneth will be on cloud nine!"

"Don't say anything until after Donald talks to him."

"I won't. Can I tell John?"

"Sure."

SILENT KNIGHT

The following evening, the Colonel answered the door and invited Kenneth Pendleton inside. The young man looked squeaky clean and was wearing a fresh white shirt, navy blue slacks, and a beat up pair of sneakers. His brown hair was freshly cut, probably by his mother, and carefully combed. He was nervous.

The Knight extended his hand and Kenneth shook it.

"Kenneth, I am so glad to finally meet you. I have heard very good things about you from John Conrady, my former Squire, and Mr. Ramsey."

"John and Mr. Ramsey are very kind."

"As you know, you have been recommended by Mr. Lucas to be my next Squire. Together we can do much good."

"My mother told me you had spoken with her."

The two had walked into the living room. Kenneth's attention was devoted to the Colonel. He appeared oblivious to the house or the surroundings. In fact, he hung on every word the Colonel said and kept his gaze on the Colonel's face.

Kenneth's thoughts were racing. Who is this man? Why is he interested in me? Is he the one that paid for my ring? Does he know what the Silent Knights have done for me? Am I good enough to be a Squire?

He looked at the Colonel and liked his face. The eyes looked sharp and the wrinkles around them indicated years of exposure to the ele-

141

ments. The lines on his face were mostly from smiling or peering into the sun. The face had a kind quality about it. His style was gracious and open but concealed a power, a disciplined toughness. Kenneth figured this was not a man you would want as an enemy. There was steel in the eyes, beneath layers of charm. This was a gentleman by choice, and a warrior by trade. Kenneth thought this was important to remember.

Kenneth had seen this man from a distance at football games, local community gatherings, school concerts, etc., but he had never met him. He had only known that Colonel Peterson had a good reputation as a retired military officer, Good Samaritan, and that he and his wife were colorful social figures. They were active and a little eccentric.

The Colonel was puzzled by this youngster: Kenneth was not what he expected. He was far more focused than Donald had expected. His face was hard, the eyes were curious and the handshake was firm. There was something about him that seemed out of reach. Kenneth had a cold spirit, an aloofness. The Colonel thought that Kenneth was not going to be an easy person to get to know. Could Kenneth be this way because of years of self-protection? Distance is a means of dealing with pain; avoidance works, but it is a large roadblock to spiritual growth. Yes, Kenneth had far to go, but they would get there together.

Helena entered the living room with fresh

SILENT KNIGHT

baked cookies, coffee and some chocolate candies. "Would you care for a soda or iced tea instead of coffee?"

Kenneth looked at Helena. "No, thank you, ma'am. I believe the coffee will be fine. I have been drinking coffee since I started school. Mom always makes a pot in the mornings. We drink coffee or water in our home."

Helena smiled and said. "Well you are easy to please." She sat beside her husband.

"Yes, ma'am." Kenneth took a cookie from the plate and bit into it.

Donald said, "Kenneth, if you agree to be my Squire, we will do much good for people in the community."

"What will I do?"

"You will deliver items to people in need. It can range from lettermen's jackets for school kids that could not afford them to cash, depending on the situation. Your primary job will be to keep me anonymous."

Kenneth responded. "That is why the motto of the Silent Knights is Psalm 115."

"Precisely, Kenneth. Not unto us, O Lord, not unto us, but to Thy name give glory."

"Sir, I must tell you that I have received some gifts from the Silent Knights. I guess I am considered one of those in need."

"Then you know how we operate and have benefited from random acts of charity. This may have better prepared you for service as a Squire."

Kenneth had not thought of it that way. "Sir,

SILENT KNIGHT

I don't have nice clothes or transportation of my own. My family just gets by."

"Kenneth, there will be no cost to you as my Squire, and I will never do anything to embarrass you."

Kenneth looked unsettled. "Sir, the best clothes I own are the ones I am wearing. I don't even have a pair of dress shoes. I may not "fit" in."

"Kenneth, you are not here because of what you wear, you are here because of your potential for leadership, good character and reputation. The clothing is minor; however, we will take care of you first. I think a good pair of shoes, a few dress shirts, a nice blazer, a couple of ties and a few pairs of slacks will be a good start. What do you think?"

Kenneth was dumbfounded. "Sir, I wasn't asking for anything."

"I know, but Helena and I will be happy to outfit a Squire with your potential. Anyway, you will need them later for college, if all goes well."

"Sir, college is not in the cards for me. My family can't afford it."

"Kenneth, we are going to work with you to find student loans or scholarships when the time comes. Education isn't hard to pay for if you demonstrate the potential necessary to pay it off."

Kenneth was in disbelief. "You are serious?"

"Of course I am. You don't know how important you are or how much potential you have. Over the next year, Helena and I intend to show you." The Knight looked at his bride, smiled and winked.

Kenneth looked at Helena; she had a lovely smile and the deepest eyes he had ever seen. He looked at the Colonel and said nothing; he couldn't think of anything to say at a moment like this.

The Colonel leaned toward him and said. "Kenneth, do you want to be my Squire?"

Kenneth took a deep breath and smiled a big sheepish grin and said. "Yes, Sir. I would be proud to be your Squire."

"Outstanding!"

The Colonel and Helena shared a pleased look at each other and both patted Kenneth on the back.

The Colonel reached into his pocket and produced a lapel pin. Kenneth gazed at the pin and smiled as the Knight affixed it to the pocket of his shirt.

"Now, you are in uniform. This pin serves to remind you of what you represent. Chivalry and Christian values are what we are all about. You should act in a way that makes those you represent proud."

The Colonel explained the meaning of chivalry and the three talked for a couple of hours about the Order, being a Christian, doing good, and former Squires.

They agreed to meet on Saturday for a shopping spree.

As Kenneth departed he said, "Sir Donald, I

hope to make you proud."

Donald said. "You just did."

The following Saturday morning, Kenneth arrived at the Petersons wearing the same clothes he had worn the first evening they had met. They enjoyed a continental breakfast that Helena had prepared.

Helena asked, "Kenneth, do you have any color preferences or style of clothing you would like?"

"No, ma'am. I don't know anything about clothes. Never had a dress coat or a tie. If you can make me look as distinguished as the Colonel did at the band concert last year, that would be neat."

"That is a very nice compliment, Kenneth. I have never had a Squire that wanted to look like me."

"Well, I don't want to look that old."

Helena nearly spit coffee all over the table. She had been mid-sip when Kenneth made his verbal faux pas. She looked at her Knight while she leaned over her plate drying the coffee off her chin.

Sir Donald said nothing but had a great expression of disbelief on his face.

Kenneth started trying to recover, "Sir, I didn't mean you were old... I meant... ummm... ahhhhh..."

Helena burst into uncontrolled laughter and was now snorting for breath between serious uncontrolled outbreaks. This caused Kenneth to start laughing at Helena. The whole scene became a cycle. Helena would snort and beat her hands on the table, Kenneth would burst into laughter and the Colonel alternated between looking at each of them and shaking his head. The process lasted for about five cycles.

Finally, Helena got composed and Kenneth waited for the Colonel to say something.

Helena started, "Putzi, you aren't old..." She didn't get it all out before she lost it again. Of course, Kenneth fell right in.

The Colonel, after watching this scene for another thirty seconds, carefully folded his napkin. He rose from the table and feigned disgust as he looked down on them, "Kenneth, you may go home now. Helena, go to your room. I am going shopping." Donald laughed and shook his head as he walked to the front door.

Both Helena and Kenneth followed the Colonel to the car. For sure, Helena and Kenneth had bonded.

Kenneth asked, "What is this business with "Putzi"?"

As the door to the garage opened, Helena lost it again.

The men's wholesale store was well stocked and Helena had taken over as the fashion master. The first step was shoes: black loafers that could be used for casual or dress occasions. Then six pairs of black socks were added. Next were measurements for pants and shirts. After a plain black leather belt matching the shoes was found, three dress shirts were added to the collection.

147

SILENT KNIGHT

Helena looked like an artist working her canvas. Kenneth was her palette and she was going to create a masterpiece. There were three sales people catering to her as she called for an assortment of colors and styles of blazers and pants. She was into it, and the Colonel was enjoying the show.

So far, Kenneth was being draped with this and that coat or color but he had not tried on anything. He seemed to be in the middle of a swirling mass of materials and had no control in the events. Kenneth wasn't complaining, he just couldn't believe what was happening. Helena would call for a color or a specific style and stuff would appear, sales people would drape him while Helena would look and either immediately say "no" or turn to the Colonel for a nod or shake of his head. Kenneth had never experienced anything like it.

After Helena chose several blazers and pants of different colors, she ordered Kenneth to go try on one outfit at a time. As he would reappear, the Colonel and Helena would pick a tie and the Colonel would tie it for Kenneth and have him try it on. The transformation was amazing. Kenneth couldn't help himself. He would look at his new reflection in the mirror and it felt soooooo good!

Finally, the choices were made. Kenneth ended up with a navy blue blazer, four pairs of pants; one pair in navy blue to create a suit, and a tan, white, and slate gray pair to extend the wardrobe. Three shirts and three ties were also selected in multiple colors. The total bill was just over $400. The effect on Kenneth was beyond calculating. "Cinderfella" was now a prince.

That evening, as the Colonel and Helena sat in their living room, they listened to an album by Miles Davis while sipping Grand Marnier. They replayed the events of the day and reveled in the fun they had had. Kenneth was in happy shock when he had departed.

The Colonel chuckled and looked at Helena, "Sometimes... clothes really do make the man."

SILENT KNIGHT

CHAPTER 15

This was the fastest year of the Petersons' lives. Kenneth had developed into a super Squire. Dozens of families had benefited over the year from his considerable efforts. He was a fine young man and West Point would be proud to have him, along with John Conrady the next Fall. It had taken every "blue chip" Mr. Ramsey and the Colonel had, but both Squires were accepted. Patti had received a partial scholarship to Baylor University, a Baptist school in Texas. Since it appeared that all three would be leaving the area and few opportunities would exist for the Petersons and their charges to get together again, Helena and the Colonel prepared a special private dinner for their three friends.

Their charges arrived promptly at seven. It was a casual evening and the men wore khakis with knit shirts while Patti wore black slacks and a bright red silk blouse. Helena sported a colorful red, blue and gold Thai silk pantsuit with a matching tunic that flowed as she breezed through the house.

The Colonel had prepared a rib eye roast marinated in Worchestershire sauce and pepper. It was cooked at high temperature,

SILENT KNIGHT

wrapped in a rock salt flour dough. The flavor and juices were sealed in the meat as the dough hardened. The dough turned a deep brown with sharp black salt protruding from the dark crust. The Colonel had not told the young guests what was to be served... it was a surprise he was about to spring.

He invited everyone into the kitchen to show them their special dinner. All had eaten meals with the Petersons before and knew that whatever it was, it would be delicious, so expectations were high.

As the group crowded around the oven to see the chef's masterpiece they were all primed to render accolades... just as the Colonel had hoped. When he opened the oven the group started a high-pitched "Oooooooohhhhhhhhh" that quickly became a low pitched "UUUUUUUUHHHHHHH???" as the tray was pulled into view, revealing something that looked more like a meteorite than a delicacy.

The Colonel toyed with the group with great enjoyment. He had achieved the exact reaction he had desired. Helena had seen this scene played out before and was watching with quiet amusement. As the Colonel set the tray on the kitchen center island cutting board in full view of the guests, he pulled a mallet from the overhead rack. The young folks were really curious now.

The Knight smacked the top of the dough, breaking the seal. Steam poured forth, filling the room with a heavenly aroma that made everyone utter another high pitched, "Oooooooohhhhhhh!" As the meat was hoisted onto the serving platter, the dough and salt fell away, revealing a perfectly cooked roast that was so tender it could be cut with a fork.

Kenneth said, "I may miss this part of Squire duty more than anything else."

John smiled and said, "I can identify with that sentiment."

Helena asked everyone to move to the dining room so she could assemble the remaining courses. She playfully shooed the group out of the kitchen. Patti stayed behind to help the Dame and to chat.

The Colonel joined his charges at the dining room table where they chatted, joked and laughed while awaiting the first course. John turned the conversation toward a more serious discussion when he asked, "Sir, from the perspective of your thirty years of military service, what advice would you give a new officer?"

The Knight pondered the question a moment before saying. "There is so much to learn. There is no simple answer, but our nation is experiencing a long break from deadly conflict. Our citizens do not appreciate the military in peacetime and our politicians tend to bleed it financially at the expense of training and maintenance. It creates dangerous conditions for those serving. You and Kenneth must remember that an Army exists to fight and win wars. Even a small peace keeping or nation building mission can be quite dangerous. Never forget

SILENT KNIGHT

that you are responsible to train your soldiers like their lives depend on it... because it does. Soldiering is serious business."

"Beyond that, an officer's primary job is to empower his people to do their job. Don't tell them how to do it. Tell them what needs to be done, ask them what they need to accomplish the mission and focus on providing that support."

The Colonel was deep in thought and smiled at some distant memory.

"Let them amaze you with their initiative and imagination. My soldiers never failed me because they valued the trust and confidence that I placed in them. Soldiers develop an incredible sense of group loyalty in that kind of environment."

The Colonel bent forward and gazed thoughtfully at the young men before continuing. "Always remember to compliment your people and never take the credit for their work. Any commander or supervisor you have, who's worth a nickel, will know you did your job, and proper rewards will come to you in the long run."

He shifted his focus to look directly into John's eyes. "Never tolerate dishonesty, unsafe training or immoral conduct... and never reward lapses in integrity. Hypocrisy is a cancer to any organization."

Sir Donald leaned back still thinking about the advice. He smiled and chuckled. "You will learn quickly that common sense isn't common. A soldier can tear up an anvil... given a toothpick and time. Nothing is soldier-proof."

"You must remember to underwrite honest mistakes or your people will be afraid to act decisively."

The Colonel looked at the two young men and knew he had given too long an answer. "You will appreciate this advice far more after a few years in the military."

Kenneth looked pensive. "It doesn't sound too hard..."

The Knight looked at Kenneth. "No... leadership is very demanding. What I just told you may sound simple; however, it is very difficult to do. Being consistent with the justice you dispense, regardless of the rank of the person involved, creates trust in you... but it will bring you into intense conflict from all sides. Enforcing standards and holding people accountable is tough business... even in peacetime."

The Colonel smiled at the young men in a knowing way. "In five years, we should meet and decide whether it was so simple. I would like to hear your thoughts then."

The old Knight leaned back and smiled at his squires.

Helena appeared from the kitchen carrying a large serving bowl with a colorful salad. It was time to eat and all were surrounded by the aroma of a pending feast.

The conversation was good, the atmosphere was jovial and the Knight and Dame tried to share the exuberance of their young friends

SILENT KNIGHT

about their eminent departure for a new life adventure. Donald and Helena were both holding their own emotions in check. Only the elders can understand the value of youthful friends... for youth is a spring that provides inner joy, excitement and hopeful dreams with great expectations.

The Knight was sixty-seven and feared loneliness more than death... although he would never admit that. His bride was his harbor and the Squires were the wind in his sails. He loved his bride and his role as a Silent Knight and wished that evenings like this would never end. Donald believed with all his heart that being a good husband, a role model and a trusted friend is about as good a legacy as anyone could hope for.

The evening ended with gifts for each of the guests. All three received identical gold necklaces with the Templar cross, suspended from a crown affixed to the chain. The gifts were not extravagant, just a gentle reminder of distant friends who would always be there for them.

Patti cried.

Helena patted her Maiden on the arm. "You were my first Maiden. You will always be very special to me. You taught me so much."

Patti shook her head and responded. "I will always love you."

They both cried while the men watched in typical male isolation from moments of tender female emotion. Secretly each wished they had the freedom to be so vocal; however, men are different, especially Knights.

There was one surprise left for the evening. John excused himself from the table. When he returned, he held a flat, medium size box. He handed it to the colonel.

"Sir Donald and Dame Helena, the three of us have a gift for you. We know you did not expect anything, nor want anything from us except our friendship, but we wanted to do something special for both of you."

Sir Donald passed the gift to his bride. "You open it, Dear."

Helena gently unwrapped the box and withdrew a highly varnished walnut plaque with twenty brass plates affixed to it. On each of the plates was the name of a Squire and the one Maiden, and beside each name their time of service was engraved. At the top, in large script engraved into the wood, was the motto, "NOT UNTO US, O LORD, NOT UNTO US, BUT TO THY NAME GIVE GLORY."

It was beautiful. It was hung in the entry of the Petersons' home for the rest of their lives... and only God knew that only eight more names would be added.

SILENT KNIGHT

SILENT KNIGHT

CHAPTER 16

Fourteen years had passed since that sweet parting, when a cold, tired, and frustrated, Major John Conrady, Battalion Executive Officer of 5th Battalion, 7th Air Defense Artillery, in Bitburg, Germany, was summoned to the headquarters by the Sergeant Major.

The young officer entered the headquarters wearing his battle dress camouflage uniform and dirty combat boots. It was a typical rainy, early fall day in the Eifel. His field cap and rainproof field jacket were still in place as he spoke into the cellular phone.

"Chief, I don't care if the brakes are O.K., we aren't putting it on the road till both brake lights work. This is peacetime, not war. No sense in risking a life over a brake light." With a black-gloved finger he push the "END" button.

The Sergeant Major, Gregory Downing, a forty-year-old African American soldier of considerable size and impression, stood as the young officer entered the office and said, "Sir, I wouldn't have interrupted you, but your father is on the phone. He says it is important, and wanted to hold until you could get here; it doesn't sound good."

SILENT KNIGHT

The Sergeant Major shook his head and looked at the floor.

The young Major's mind raced. Was it his mother? Had someone had an accident? It was uncommon for his father to call at work. As a matter of fact, it was the first time it had occurred.

"Thanks, Sergeant Major. I'll take it in my office."

John walked into his office, shut the door and moved behind his desk. He slumped into the executive swivel chair before picking up the phone and punching the blinking light. He tossed his cap haphazardly toward the couch.

"Hello, Dad. It's John. Is everything OK?

"Your mom and I are fine, but we just got word that Colonel Peterson is very sick, he had a check-up and has been diagnosed with cancer. He went too long without going to the doctor and it has progressed badly."

The news hit John like an indictment. He had only seen the Knight twice since the dinner fourteen years ago and had only called a couple of times. He sent a Christmas card... when he got them out... but he knew he had been a poor friend to the Petersons. He had always intended to stay in touch or to make a special trip to see the old Knight. Now it might be too late.

"How is Helena?"

"She is OK. Tells everyone that Putzi needs their prayers. You know she would never complain."

SILENT KNIGHT

John thought about what to do. He should go see his friend. His conscience was doing a number on him. The thought immediately sprang to his mind that he had to tell the old Knight that he loved him. He had never done that, and he needed to.

"Dad, what hospital is he in?"

"John, you know Donald: he isn't in a hospital, he is at home. When the doctors told him he had only six weeks to live, he just asked that they help him make it as painless as possible, but he was going home. He isn't taking any extraordinary measures to lengthen his life. He says he has known his Lord too long to be afraid of joining Him."

John straightened in his chair and leaned forward. There was a long pause as he thought about the Colonel. "Dad, the Colonel is going to die just like he lived... with dignity... and he is going to demonstrate courage."

John's dad was silent.

The young Major was now in the grip of fear. He had to call his old friend but what would he say? Could he see him before he died? He wasn't due a leave till Christmas and that was three months away. If the Colonel only had six weeks he would never see him again. The thought was agonizing to him. How could he have been such a poor friend to this man who had meant so much to him?

"Dad, I know I should have it, but what is the Petersons' phone number?"

His father gave him the number and said,

SILENT KNIGHT

"John, if you call, I don't know what you will say, but tell them I said thank you. I don't know if I could do it myself. Your mother and I sent flowers and a card."

John's eyes began to fill with tears and a lump formed in his throat. He choked out, "Dad, I'll tell them."

The lump in the young officer's throat grew as he stammered out, "gotta go, Dad... love you."

"Love you, too, son. Don't wait too long to call. I don't think the Colonel will be with us much longer."

John had tears streaming down his face as he returned the phone to its cradle.

Memories crowded into the young officer's brain. Discussions about integrity, dignity, character and courage sprang forth as if summoned by some great military order. His mind swirled in the memory of the warmth of a distant friendship.

He sat leaning on his desk, looking at the phone number but could not bring himself to punch the numbers. He picked up the receiver and listened to the dial tone. The pain was too great, the indictment too strong. He decided to wait till after work to make the call from home. His emotions were too sharp to deal with this situation, especially when anyone might walk in. After all, he was a Major in the U.S. Army: too tough to let his men know he could be this sensitive. The thought of someone walking in and seeing him now mortified him. He rose from his chair, straightened his battle dress uniform, grabbed his cap and wiped his eyes as he headed out the door to inspect his unit. John was glad to have something else to occupy his thoughts.

That evening, upon returning to his austere bachelor's officer quarters, he stripped off the tunic throwing it on the couch as he stepped into the small kitchenette for a cold beer. He would need two before gaining the courage to call the Petersons. He must have paced a mile between his kitchen and the living room before deciding he had hesitated long enough. It is strange how the mind can turn guilt into an unlimited series of potential outcomes to any situation. John's fear was that the Petersons would be angry with him and say something negative about his thoughtlessness. He moved to his favorite chair and picked up the phone.

As he dialed the last digit, he prayed the Petersons line would be busy. The overseas call took several seconds to connect but the line was free. Helena answered.

"Hello."

"Helena, this is John Conrady calling from Germany."

John was not prepared for the excitement in the voice that responded.

"Oh, John, we have been so worried about you. Thank God you called! You have no idea how important this call is to Putzi and me."

John immediately thought how ironic it was

SILENT KNIGHT

that the Petersons would be worried about him instead of being focused on their own situation. It was so typical of them. He felt ashamed for the miscalculation and hesitation in calling his old friends.

"Helena, I heard that the Colonel was ill."

There was a pause... then Helena responded, "Putzi is not well. He is resting but he is not in pain."

"I hope to see him soon."

There was a longer pause. John heard in his mind words not spoken. "It should be soon, John. Putzi would appreciate that very much."

John's throat began to knot. Tears began to stream down his face again. It was embarrassing even though he was alone. He rose from the well-worn overstuffed chair and shuffled to the middle of the room mindlessly whipping the phone cable. His chest became tight; words were hard to form now. "Helena, how soon do I need to be there, to speak to him?"

Helena's voice quivered. "Soon, John... very soon. I fear he won't stay coherent much longer with the medication he is receiving."

"I must tell him something."

Helena said with a measured tone, "Speak to him now."

John couldn't believe it. He hadn't counted on talking to the Colonel over the phone. This was so personal, and a telephone call just didn't seem right. Yet, who was he to choose the moment. He had not been the friend he should have. Once again, he was in a situation not of his choosing. The Colonel seemed to expand John's emotional experience every time they met. Why should this be any different? John's mind reeled at the challenge.

"Helena, God bless you and the Colonel. I feel so bad for not having been a better friend."

The response was immediate. "John, how could you say such a thing. We love you. You have always been special to us."

Tears continued to flow from John's eyes. Helena's words were not meant to hurt, but they struck like a knife into his soul. He couldn't possibly decline to speak to the Colonel, but this would be a moment he would never forget.

"Helena, I never told him..." the words hung in his throat. "I love him."

It took forever for Helena to respond. Her voice was more constricted than he had ever heard, "You should speak to him now. It is important." The words trailed off in a desperate gasp and John could hear the phone on Helena's end hit the counter as she set it down. He knew that in seconds he would be speaking to his friend... perhaps his best friend, for the last time. He still didn't know how to say what needed to be said.

After several minutes, a familiar voice, much stronger than John had anticipated sounded through the receiver. "John... John. Thank God you called. I have been so concerned about you."

It was all John could do to maintain control

SILENT KNIGHT

of his battered emotions. "Sir, I understand it is I that should be worried about you."

The immediate response came back, "God and Helena are caring for me. I can't ask for more. Don't worry about me, I am prepared to meet my Lord. Will I see you again?"

John was stunned by the crisp and businesslike reply, the steadiness from a man near death. "Sir, I hope to see you soon... but I wanted to tell you...."

The words hung in his throat, his chest burned and he feared he would lose his grip on his emotions completely. His strength failed him. He dropped to his knees in the middle of his living room. The young man choked out, "Thank you for everything you have done for me... and... I love you."

There was a long silence on the other end. John moved the phone away from his face and held his free hand over his mouth so his sobbing could not be heard... but he could hear Colonel Peterson sobbing on the other end. It was more than he could bear.

After a full minute of silence, a different voice responded. It was the Colonel but all pretense of strength had been stripped away. A choked, whispered message burned in John's ear. "I love you, John... I hope to see you soon. You don't know how much I appreciate you calling."

The phone went silent for another full minute. Helena's voice was back.

"John, thank you for calling. Putzi is overwhelmed by your call and he needs to rest."

John squeaked out, "I understand. I will see you soon."

"I hope so. It would be so good."

"I love you, Helena."

"I love you too, John." Her voice was very strained. "I have to go."

"Goodnight."

The phone clicked off.

SILENT KNIGHT

CHAPTER 17

It had been seven weeks since the phone call with Helena. The young Major had juggled many important training requirements to take leave now. News from home was not good. His father had told him that Donald had slipped in and out of consciousness the previous week and was no longer eating. Time was not in his favor.

Flying military, space available, commonly referred to as "Space A," was a challenge in itself but this was still off-season for vacationing military families. Thanksgiving was two weeks away and schools were still in session. John was able to get manifested on the first flight of the day to the United States. The C-17 flight that originated from Ramstein, Germany, was long but only cost six dollars, and that was for the box lunch. The cold chicken, apple and potato chips were hardly comforting. Major Conrady was tired and suffered from morbid thoughts about his friend's impending death. Guilt and despair tugged at his consciousness. He didn't fight it, he wallowed in it and felt he deserved it. The "John Wayne" machismo that suited his leadership style was crumbling under the truth of his vulnerability and vanity.

SILENT KNIGHT

He had finally met a situation the Colonel and his Army training had not prepared him to handle or separate himself from, emotionally. The two possibilities terrified him equally: first, that he might make it to see the Colonel before he died and second, that he might not make it in time.

If he made it prior to the Colonel's death, there was too much to say. If he made it too late, there would be things left unsaid. He had packed his dress blues for the funeral, in case the Colonel didn't last through his visit. It was an appropriate tribute to another soldier; however, the thought made John feel hollow. The flight to Dover Air Force Base, Delaware, seemed to last forever. It touched down safely at sixteen hundred hours (four o'clock civilian time).

Once in Dover, he rented a car and drove the three hours to the Petersons. He stopped to purchase flowers, freshen up and grab a hamburger on the outskirts of Washington, DC. His navy blazer looked a little wrinkled from the trip, but he carefully pulled the Squire lapel pin from his pocket and pinned it near the buttonhole. He had treasured the pin and never saw it that it didn't bring a fond memory and a smile with it. Today, it did little to raise his spirits.

He was thankful to find a good music station on the car radio. The trip would have been unbearable without it. His thoughts were too morbid and nothing he did seemed to shake the darkness within him.

The Petersons' house looked as he remembered it, but there were a half dozen cars parked on the street and in the driveway. Obviously, several of the Petersons' friends were visiting... or he was too late. As he parked in the familiar driveway, his thoughts ran back to the first time he had visited this home. He had been just as frightened; only he wished the situation were the same now.

He didn't know what to expect. How would the Colonel look? What would he say?

He approached the house and was halfway up the walk when the big oak front door swung open and Helena, now white-haired and stately, briskly strode to meet him. She still looked elegant... almost regal. They hugged immediately and held it for a long tender moment.

"John, it is so good to see you." She looked at his face as if for the first time. She seemed to be memorizing every new wrinkle. "You are even more handsome than I remembered." Her hand swept through his dark hair in that charming way of hers. "The Army has been good to you."

John looked into Helena's eyes and saw the sorrow and red from crying. "Is Sir Donald..."

The question was never finished. Helena said, "He has been waiting to see you. Your father called this morning and said you would be here today."

As they entered the house arm in arm, John

handed the flowers to Helena saying, "I almost forgot, these are for you."

"Thank you, after I get you back to Putzi, I will put them in water."

John tried to conceal the fear that filled his heart and mind, of being alone with his friend.

As they walked through the living room, John recognized several of the guests and hesitated as if he were going to stop and chat. Helena spoke to the assembled group, "You all may visit with John after he has seen Putzi."

As they entered the hallway John could see the old Knight through the open door to the bedroom at the far end. His profile was gaunt, his eyes were open but focused on the ceiling; his mouth sagged open. Ruprecht, now a very old dog, lay beside the bed. His tail wagged a couple of times as Helena approached.

The next thing that happened would haunt John for the rest of his life.

The gaunt figure turned his head to watch the approaching couple. They were probably twenty-five feet from his door. The eyes were dark and sunk into the sockets. Despite the look of death, a smile shaped on the drawn lips and a voice struggled to say, "Squire... where... have you been? I have... been waiting for you."

The Colonel's appearance stopped John in his tracks. Helena pulled his arm forward and John tried to steel himself mentally and emotionally. The young officer felt that he was no longer in control. He was being swept along by events.

SILENT KNIGHT

As they entered the room, the old Knight lifted his hand to shake John's. The grip was gone, but the eyes, deep within the well of their sockets, still had a flicker of life in them.

John was speechless; he leaned over and kissed the Colonel on his forehead. "Sir, it is good to see you again." The words sounded stupid the moment he said them. He didn't know what else to say; his mind was numb.

A familiar voice from behind said. "Well, do Majors have hugs for old girl friends?"

John turned to see a beautiful woman wearing a perfectly tailored navy blue dress that accentuated the curves of a well-proportioned figure. It was Patti. She was ravishing. John was too stunned to speak; his senses were overloaded. "Well....ah... of course."

She moved into his arms and hugged him tightly. Patti whispered. "We are so thankful you made it here in time."

Helena took Patti by the arm and said. "Let's leave the boys alone for awhile." She turned to John. "Call us if you need anything." She turned to the Colonel and said with a wink and a smile. "You play nice with the children and don't run off."

The door closed behind them and John pulled a straight back chair to the bedside. As he sat, the Colonel seized his hand and held it. His other hand slowly moved across his frail body and stopped on top of the Major's hand. His eyes looked as if there were many things to say, excited and somehow pleading. No words were exchanged for a few moments. The Colonel was working hard to form the words in his mind.

Ruprecht stood slowly, stretched a little and sniffed John's hand. The dog moved to his side, sat and put his head in John's lap where he could be patted.

Donald said in a raspy, weak voice. "Can't talk long; too weak. You must... listen closely." His breathing was labored.

"Yes, Sir."

"No time left."

"Sir, I am not good at bedside manners. I won't sit here and tell you things will get better. We've known each other too long to lie to each other."

"Thank you. Never could... suffer liars... or thieves." He managed a small smile.

"Are you scared?"

"Yes."

"Do you want to talk about it?"

"Yes. I'd like that."

"Are you frightened of death?

"No. I worry... for Helena... God and I... we're friends... have been... long time." The old man was doing all he could.

"Sir, you have many friends, Helena will be well cared for." John hesitated, "I will be a better friend to her than I have been to you." He lowered his head averting his eyes from the old Knight's gaze. "I promise."

"John... don't be... hard on yourself. You have made... proud... us... proud." Slowly, the

SILENT KNIGHT

Colonel gently patted John's hand.

Tears welled up in the Major's eyes.

The old Knight continued to talk, struggling for breath between words. "Our job... was to... encourage... you. You flew... away... high."

John interrupted, "You gave me the courage and the confidence to succeed."

The old Knight sighed, relaxed a little, smiled and said. "Then the... lesson is... complete."

"Sir, what do you mean?"

"You understand... Squire... it was done... for you."

John choked back tears. "I understand." He struggled for his own breath. "I love you."

The Knight squeezed his hand, "I can't cry... tears don't work... anymore... love you always. Remember me... and Helena... you must... continue."

The Major was barely able to stay in the room. Emotionally he was a wreck. "Continue what?"

The Knight squeezed his hand, "Giving... you must... become a Knight... honor me."

John was overwhelmed and shook his head. "Yes. Yes. Yes, Sir. I will do that, and continue the tradition of the Silent Knight."

"Promise."

John sat there holding the Knight's hand for about ten minutes while his friend slept. He quietly wept and wiped the tears away. He was thankful no one else could see him. His nerves were raw. Ruprecht was good company at this

175

moment and appreciated the young officer's gentle strokes from his free hand.

Sir Donald's breathing had finally become steady. Ruprecht labored to wag his tail as the door quietly opened and Helena stepped in. She whispered. "How did it go?"

John struggled to speak. The lump in his throat prohibited him from replying immediately. He motioned for her to come near. Finally, he managed to say. "He wants me to become a Knight."

Helena placed her hand on his shoulder, "I know. I think it was the only thing that kept him going the last two weeks. He wanted to ask you himself. He wrote you a letter... in case. I have it for you, but you must not read it until after he is gone." She leaned over and hugged John and they both quietly wept. They sat with the old soldier and watched him sleep.

Perhaps an hour elapsed before John ventured out of the bedroom and into the living room. Helena had encouraged him to go talk to the others. He left her sitting with her Knight.

Patti was the only visitor left. She looked like she stepped out of a fashion magazine. John thought, my God, she has become a young Helena. She had all the style and grace... and a lot more if he were any judge of women.

Patti approached John with two glasses of red wine. "They have missed you. I must admit that I always wondered if I would see you again. It is unfortunate we have to meet under

SILENT KNIGHT

these circumstances. It has been too long."

"Yes." John was trying to restrain his emotions but a tear ran down his cheek. He choked out. "He wants me to become a Knight."

Patti's face radiated compassion. "I know. He has talked of little else the past three weeks. You meant more to us than you are probably aware."

John's mind was slow but he was sure she said, us. "Us?"

"Yes, us! I have never forgotten you. And if those tears mean you are still as sensitive and loving as the young man I used to know, I want to know you again."

John was surprised by her openness. "I have thought of you often. Even picked up the phone to call you... more than once."

"Why didn't you?" She sipped wine from one of the glasses and licked the liquid from her lips.

The sensuousness of the moment was not lost on John. "You are pretty bold these days."

She said. "Time is something that is slipping away. I have learned that... if nothing else... from the past two months in this home. My time is running out... so I'll be forward with you. Are you married?"

"No." John was amazed by her bravado. "Never had a serious relationship since we parted." It was the truth.

"Many unserious relationships?"

"Too many to discuss." That was a lie. "What about you?"

"Never married. No children." She grinned. "Only two serious prospects."

"Oh. How is that?" John was curious now.

"My latest boy friend is an attorney, very wealthy and unfortunately, self-centered, and he thinks everything can be solved with money. He wants to marry me and shower me with riches." She pouted.

"Sounds terrible." John managed his first smile of the evening.

She bristled, "Don't you laugh at me, John Conrady! I haven't answered him... yet."

"What's keeping you?"

"The second prospect."

"And what would that be?"

Patti's eyes broke contact with his. She stared at the wine glasses in her hands.

"Maybe you." She sighed and shook her head. "Maybe it is just memories of you and happier, simpler times. I had a dream once, but somewhere along the way it got lost. The most meaningful times I have had in my life, I had with you and the Petersons." Patti looked up with a pained, searching expression. "I want it back... if I can get it. Do you remember those days?"

John was mesmerized by the woman Patti had become. In his eyes, she was bold, alluring and sensitive. He could feel himself melting in her presence. "Yes, I remember. I have never been the same. My days as a Squire changed me permanently... and frankly, I don't know how I am going to handle this loss."

SILENT KNIGHT

"I know how you feel. I feel the same way. We will face it together." She looked at the floor.

"You are beautiful. You have grown into a young Helena."

She looked up. "Thank you. That is a great compliment... but I don't think Helena was ever in a situation like this." Patti smiled self-consciously.

"Are you going to drink both those glasses of wine?"

"I didn't know if you would want wine. I brought this for Helena. It's from my vineyard."

"Are you serious? You have a vineyard?"

"Yes. It's a long story." She smiled, batted her eyes, and flirted. "Would you like to share a glass with me?"

John looked into her eyes and marveled. "Only if you tell me the whole story."

He moved close, placed his left hand on her face and pulled her gently to his. John kissed her firmly on the mouth. She responded boldly.

His heart had been swept away twice within the last two hours, once by sorrow and once by romance. He didn't know if he could handle much more. This was a turn of events that John had not considered... but he was glad to be home.

Colonel Peterson spoke with Helena for about an hour the following morning before falling into a coma. She didn't discuss his final words. He died two days later, at home, surrounded by three of his former Squires, two of Helena's Maidens, and Father Riley. Helena was holding his hand when he breathed his last. John was amazed at the peacefulness, the silence of death. It was nothing to fear.

Helena was first to realize the Colonel had gone. She simply took his wedding band from his hand and slipped it on her finger. She patted his hand and said, "Thank you, Putzi." She rose and left the room.

In the end, it was not a tragedy. It was the end of suffering. The Knight had joined his Lord.

CHAPTER 18

The Colonel's death brought a hollow feeling to all who had gathered. The apprehension of his death was balanced by a sense of relief. Nobody wanted the old soldier to die, but nobody wanted him to suffer any longer either. There was a peaceful acceptance about the whole ordeal. His friends were not "tearing their garments."

Donald's body was taken to a local funeral home and prepared. Dressed in his most formal military uniform, adorned with his awards and the Knight's Templar cross hanging from his neck, the body laid in a simple, flag-draped, Eisenhower-style casket. For two days the body was available for viewing by family and friends. Word had passed through the community quickly about the Colonel's death and his obituary had been published in several newspapers. At times, the funeral home was packed with over one hundred mourners. Viewing hours were extended to accommodate the number of people wishing to pay their respects. John was astounded by the number of mourners... it was overwhelming. A line formed outside the funeral home and did not diminish for several hours. Three books were needed to catalog the

SILENT KNIGHT

names of all the visitors.

People came from out of state. Old, young, black, brown, yellow, and white... they were all there. Many were telling a favorite story about the old soldier. Many were wanting to know if the Colonel had been the one who, as the Silent Knight, had provided this or that? There was truly no way to know.

Helena was unbelievable. She didn't cry, she didn't whimper, she met everyone that came and she always had a kind word to share. She knew most by their first name.

In some ways, it was like a reunion, especially for all the Squires.

Helena insisted on the Squires and Maidens having breakfast with her the morning of the funeral. It was an elegant catered affair. By the look of all the formal military uniforms, all Services were represented among the group. John was glad he had thought to bring his dress blues. He would have been embarrassed if he hadn't. All the civilian men were wearing dark suits and the ladies were appropriately attired in black dresses.

The table was beautifully arranged at maximum length for a buffet where everyone could serve themselves. The guests mingled as they roamed throughout the house. Former Squires ranged in age from twenty-two to fifty. They represented military, civil service, medicine, politics, ministry, banking, stock market, and social work. There was one Congressman, one Major General, two Brigadier Generals, four

Colonels, a Lieutenant Colonel, a Navy Commander, a Major, three Captains, one Catholic priest, two doctors, one Baptist minister, two bank presidents, a Secret Service agent, and others John never got around to greeting. Everyone wanted to tell favorite stories about the old Knight. The effect Colonel Peterson had had on all these men was amazing.

The former Maidens in attendance were equally impressive. The list included one Congresswoman, one Colonel, two mayors, three doctors and one charity president. Kara Clark was the current Maiden to Helena. She was a very attractive young lady with blonde hair and soft blue eyes. She flitted busily from room to room, ensuring that all in attendance were appropriately cared for while never losing sight of her Dame.

Across the living room John noticed a familiar face waving in his direction. It was Major Kenneth Pendleton looking fit, handsome and mature. From his neck hung the symbol of Knighthood. The two officers shared stories, swapped addresses and swore to stay in touch. Patti joined the young men and the time was spent talking about the profound effect their time with the Petersons had had on their lives.

About half an hour before the funeral service, the oldest Squire gathered everyone into the living room where he placed his arm around Helena. "I am moved to speak. Nobody asked me to... but I felt someone should. There is a common thread that binds each of us to-

SILENT KNIGHT

gether. I may not say it just right... so I hope you understand what my heart is trying to convey. I think that I speak for all of the former Squires and Maidens when I say that Sir Donald and Dame Helena gave us all a very special gift. Courage, compassion and confidence... these were their gifts to us... and we are now their legacy. Let us here and now pledge to carry on this legacy so that Sir Donald and Dame Helena's work never really dies. A part of them lives in all of us. What I am trying to say, Helena, is we love you and Donald."

The group raised their glasses and shouted as if planned, "Hear, hear!"

Helena was unshakable. She stepped forward, slowly wringing her hands, and said, "My, my, I hope Putzi is seeing what I am seeing right now." Her eyes swept the room, eyes that were deep and missed nothing. "He would be so pleased. You have all done so well. Our prayers for each of you have been answered abundantly. Thank you for being here. You will never know how important each one of you is to me at this moment. You are all our children."

She moved to the center of the room and looked around. "You have blessed my life and the Colonel's. Thank you."

The room erupted in cheers and applause. It lasted a full minute.

Helena held up her hand. "Now we have some business to attend to." She looked lovingly around the room. "You cannot all be pallbearers... so I am going to choose six of you to provide your services one last time for Donald. In his honor and mine, I ask all of you to understand this dilemma and not be offended. It would sadden us to think that any of you felt slighted. You are all very special to us."

The room fell totally silent.

"General Maloney... Stumpy." She smiled as she recalled the General's nickname. "You were first. You will now be last."

The General moved to stand next to Helena.

"Congressman Murphy, we worried most about you ever achieving anything." Helena managed a laugh. The entire room laughed with her. "I know you can rise to this challenge."

The Congressman wiped tears away while moving to stand next to the General.

"Colonel Leppard... Turtle. You are next." Everyone laughed but the real joke was on Helena. She never understood the nickname was really Turdle.

"Captain Pendleton... Andy." She nodded and smiled.

"Dr. Williford, you were always there, through thick and thin. You should be there for this."

"Father Pilsner, if you would be so kind?"

He responded, "It would be an honor."

The last pallbearer will be our last and youngest Squire, Fred Fay.

The twenty-two-year-old moved forward and took his place among the others.

John secretly was crushed that he had not

SILENT KNIGHT

been chosen.

Helena said, "There is one more duty that must be performed. The ritual of the cape must not be forgotten. All of you who have been Knighted into the Order should wear your cape to the funeral, consistent with our tradition. One former Squire or a serving Knight must carry the Colonel's cape behind the pallbearers and place it on top of the casket after the flag is removed. The cape is to be buried on top of the casket."

"Finally, our lamb, the one that barely made it... but made a huge difference for Donald and me." Helena held out her hand to John. "Major Conrady... John, you will carry Donald's cape."

John moved through the crowd to grasp Helena's hands and then moved to stand with the group. He had never been so proud... or so humbled. He was too choked to say anything. The act of placing the Knight's cape on the casket prior to burial was the modern equivalent of placing the Knight on his shield. It was a deeply moving tradition.

Helena looked around the room at each of the faces. "Shortly, we must all move to the church; I may not see all of you together again." She motioned to the men in the center of the room. "I need the seven here to stay behind for a few moments. The rest of you I ask to meet us at the church. We will proceed from there to the cemetery for a short graveside service." She bowed her head and held up a trembling hand, the only evidence of her inner pain.

SILENT KNIGHT

She choked out, "Thank you for being part of our lives. Go now."

The house emptied in a few moments amidst the sounds of muffled whispers, soft sobs, sniffing and nose blowing.

After the room had cleared, Helena briefly explained the funeral procession plans for entering and exiting the church. The pallbearers and casket would lead the procession in and out. She would follow John, who would be six paces behind the casket carrying the cape draped over his left arm. He would sit with Helena. At the graveside service, the military honor guard would fold the American flag and present it to Helena. Once the flag exchanged hands, that would be John's signal to move forward and place the folded cape with the cross centered lengthwise on the casket. He had to ensure that the top of the cross was toward the Knight's head.

Helena decided that all seven former Squires would ride with her behind the hearse in the chauffeured limousine.

When they arrived, John was startled by the number of Knights and Dames wearing their capes. There must have been over one hundred and fifty... but that was only about a quarter of the crowd. The church was packed to standing room only. The crowd represented every corner of the community, all ages and every race. It was astounding.

There were no flowers except a simple spray from Helena. Word had been passed that the

SILENT KNIGHT

family requested that instead of flowers, donations be made to the charity of their choice, in Donald's memory.

The church service was officiated by Reverend Myers, the Peterson's Baptist preacher. It was a lovely, uncommon service. Reverend Myers behaved more like a cheerleader and referee than a preacher. The first hymn was "Trust and Obey," and it was followed by "In the Garden." These were two of Donald's favorites.

Reverend Myers opened the service with an announcement. "This is not a funeral! This is a celebration! Our friend, Donald, was ready for this moment. He had prepared for it his entire life. I am certain he has heard already the wonderful words, WELL DONE FAITHFUL SERVANT. He has known the Lord and served him well."

Several people came forward to tell hysterical stories about Sir Donald. Among them were Father Riley, Mr. Lucas, Mr. Ramsey and Mr. Keelor. John could not remember hearing so much laughter in church anywhere, much less at a funeral. As he glanced over his shoulder, John noticed Patti seated nearby. In a very strange way, the funeral was fun. It was uplifting. By the end of the service, few people were crying; most were smiling.

The closing hymn was "The Old Rugged Cross." The recessional was, of course, "Onward Christian Soldiers."

On the trip to the cemetery, John noticed that only he and the youngest Squire were not

SILENT KNIGHT

wearing capes. John couldn't help commenting that he had just become a postulant, recommended for Knighthood by the Colonel. This prompted the youngest Squire to ask. "Do you think I will ever get that opportunity?"

In unison Helena and all six of the others responded. "You wouldn't have been a Squire if Sir Donald didn't think so."

They all looked at each other and laughed.

The graveside service had about three hundred in attendance. Most of the Knights and Dames were present.

It was a glorious fall day. There was a little overcast but no precipitation. The air had a slight chill and the foliage had turned bright colors. The pallbearers performed their duties. Father Riley gave the final eulogy. It was a beautiful farewell to a brother in Christ. The closing prayer was short but more intimate than John had ever heard. Father Riley must have spent hours preparing it.

Taps was played flawlessly. The military honor guard, provided by the nearest installation, was well rehearsed and properly folded the flag. A perfectly uniformed officer stepped to Helena and handed her the flag. He bent low and said. "Please accept this flag in grateful appreciation for service to the Nation."

Helena accepted the flag and said. "Thank you and your detail. My husband would have been proud."

The young officer was moved and smartly executed a right face and moved away.

SILENT KNIGHT

John stood and carefully folded the cape. He made sure the Templar Cross was properly centered. He took three paces forward and was at the casket. He centered the cape on the casket lid, lightly ran his hand over the cross, and backed away to render a final salute. When he was seated, Father Riley asked everyone to join him in singing one stanza of "Amazing Grace."

The service ended and Helena must have stayed an hour greeting old friends. She seemed tireless.

The six pallbearers escorted Helena home while John said he would join her later. Patti had stayed behind also.

The sun was low in the sky when the gravedigger arrived on a new tractor equipped with a backhoe. The young man dismounted the tractor, took off his baseball cap and asked John if he should remove the cape before burial. John shook his head, saying, "No, it stays." The gravedigger lowered the steel casket into the ground and started to push earth on top of it. John and Patti each picked up a handful of dirt and dropped it on top of the cape. Soon it was covered and the young couple departed.

Two days later, on John's way out of town, he visited the grave. To his astonishment a headstone was already in place. It was a fairly large family headstone made of dark gray granite. The front was engraved, "HERE RESTS A SILENT KNIGHT." A quote underneath read, "Together we can do much good."

SILENT KNIGHT

The back was engraved with the Peterson's names and dates of birth. Underneath read, "They lived, they loved, they laughed, and they cared." Surprisingly, the stone had been donated by Father Riley. He had added in small letters near the base. "Donated by a friend. Father Martin Riley."

John sat on a cement bench a few yards from the grave and pulled an envelope from the breast pocket of his blazer. It was the letter from Colonel Peterson. Helena had given it to him that morning. John studied the writing on the front. It was the old Knight's hand and the writing showed the unsteadiness of age. The young Major thought, it must have taken some time to compose. He unsealed the envelope and was pleased to find the familiar SILENT KNIGHT card inside.

On the facing page was written:

John,
So sorry to have missed you. I needed to tell you that I love you. Your memory has been a treasure to me.
I learned one thing in my life and did not want you to take a lifetime to learn it, too. It is the people you love along the way that bring you happiness. The love I have given was always multiplied when it returned, and in time it always returns.
The best investment you can ever make is in other people.
Until we meet again, to His name give glory.

Forever,

SILENT KNIGHT

The letter was signed, "Your Silent Knight."

John looked up from the letter and stared at the granite tombstone. He thought to himself, "Who was this man? Why is he so important to me? What caused him to become the man he was? Where did he come from? Why did he have such magic to inspire?"

He didn't know... but he was determined to find out.

SILENT KNIGHT

SILENT KNIGHT